BAGUETTE MURDER

A Patisserie Mystery Book 3

HARPER LIN

BAGUETTE MURDER Copyright © 2014 by Harper Lin.

ISBN-13: 978-0993949517

ISBN-10: 0993949517

www.harperlin.com

CHAPTER ONE

*C*lémence Damour knew she lived a charmed life. As the heiress to the Damour patisserie chain, baking was in her blood. She spent her days developing new dessert flavors with her head baker, Sebastien Soulier, in their flagship patisserie in the 16th arrondissement; and her nights out with her friends to all the fine restaurants and bars that Paris had to offer. Aside from a few grisly murders that had happened in her neighborhood recently, things were going swimmingly. Now that she wasn't mixed up with those murder cases and Inspector Cyril St. Clair was off her back, she had more time for all the things she wanted to do, like painting.

She was just starting to get the hang of the work-life balance. Perhaps it was easier because she didn't have a boyfriend. Sure, there were a couple of guys who were interested, but Clémence found them to be wholly unsuitable. Besides, trust wasn't something that Clémence doled out easily anymore. Relationships were complicated. This was exemplified in Rose's relationship with Pierre.

Rose, whom Clémence had known since she was thirteen, had been fighting with her live-in boyfriend lately. When Rose asked Clémence to take off for a spa weekend in Switzerland, Clémence didn't hesitate. She also deserved a break after a hectic few days of trying to prove an employee's innocence in a murder case.

Rose desperately needed a break from Pierre, as he had been a curmudgeon in the past few weeks, always finding faults in whatever Rose did or said, and starting fights for no reason that she could find. Perhaps Pierre was stressed from the long hours at his finance job. He seemed to be coming home later and later in recent weeks. Nine p.m. was typical, but once in a while, he came home as late as eleven. Rose was at a breaking point. When Clémence agreed to get away on Thursday, Rose booked the trip and packed so she could leave as soon as possible when she got home from work that Friday evening.

At the Dolder Grand Hotel and Spa in Zurich, the girls spend the entire weekend getting pampered. The balcony of their suites had a stunning view of the

Alps and the lake. They received shiatsu massages with gentle tapping with bamboo to stimulate the senses, organic facials with deep pore cleansing, and they dipped in calming thermal baths and listened to meditative music. By Sunday evening, they emerged from the hotel as serene and rejuvenated as they'd ever been in their lives. Their skin was as soft as newborns', and every muscle in their bodies were relaxed.

However, on the plane back to Paris, Rose's problems began to resurface. They were flying first class and drinking champagne, but it didn't seem to assuage matters.

"We're probably going to break up," she announced.

Clémence had avoided the subject all weekend because she could see that Rose wanted to escape from her relationship troubles. Now that they were going back to Paris, back to reality, she had to face the music.

"Why do you say that?" Clémence asked. "Maybe you'll work it out."

Rose shook her head. "He has never been this nasty before. It just gets worse and worse. I have a feeling that he's being this way so he doesn't have to break up with me. He wants me to break up with him."

"You need to talk to him," Clémence said. "Maybe he's just stressed and doesn't know what he's saying half the time."

"I'm afraid to. What if there's someone else?"

"Oh Rose, don't jump to conclusions. I'm sure that if you just sit down with him, you'll get some answers. He'll either change or he won't. If you're sure that he won't, then I agree, maybe it is best to part ways."

Rose nodded meekly. "You're right. I just can't take it anymore. It's just unfortunate because we've been together for over two years. I always thought we were going to get married. I mean, we haven't talked about it, but I just assumed." She began to sob quietly so the other passengers wouldn't hear. "I wish things could go back to the way they were. He used to be so romantic in the first few months we were together—the lengths he'd go to impress me, and the presents he used to buy. And now? Nothing but meanness, insults, and taking me for granted. I do agree that his job is stressful—and it has always been stressful, but I think it's something else. He's hiding something, but I can't put my finger on it."

"Pierre doesn't seem like the type to express himself," Clémence agreed. "I don't really know him that well, to tell you the truth."

Clémence had met Pierre only a couple of times,

since she'd been away from Paris for two years to travel around the world. He was handsome in the typical Parisian way: dark haired, scruffy facial hair, well dressed, and exuding a prominent arrogance. She didn't find him entirely memorable.

"Oh, forget about this." Rose blew into her napkin. "We just had a lovely weekend, and I had to spoil the end by whining about my boyfriend."

"It's fine," Clémence said. "Sometimes it's good to take a break from each other when you're in a relationship. I'm sure it'll work itself out in the end."

"You're right. Let's get some more champagne."

The flight attendant came around with a fake smile on her face and a bottle of fine champagne in her hands. The girls got slightly toasted on the rest of the flight back. When they landed in Paris, they were giggling too loudly and annoyed the other passengers, who gave them cut eye. Their jovial mood continued as they exited the airport and got a cab—that was, until Rose called Pierre and he didn't pick up. She tried both the home number and his cell phone.

"He's not home," said Rose. "Typical. He knew I was coming home at this time. Maybe he just wants to avoid me."

"It's Sunday. Is he with his family?"

"His family lives in Lyon, and I know his parents are on vacation in Australia, so I doubt Pierre has a good excuse to be out." Her eyes widened. "What if he moved out?"

"Moved out?" Clémence turned to her.

"It's my apartment—my dad's, anyway. He let me take over the apartment when he moved to Germany. Pierre and I split the rent, and he gives me a check every month. There's nothing stopping him from just packing up to live somewhere else. The apartment was fully furnished to begin with, and Pierre doesn't have a lot of stuff."

"Rose, you're getting worked up over nothing. Pierre's probably out with friends and having a drink."

"Maybe." Rose pursed her lips. "Want to come over? I mean, until he comes back?"

Clémence had planned on picking up her dog from her friend Berenice, but she supposed Rose needed her since she was in such distress. Rose was her best friend. They had gone to the same middle school in Romainville, a suburb of Paris, and they had stayed close friends ever since. Rose was the cool, collected type, so it surprised Clémence to see her so anxious. Love brought out the monsters in people, so she must've really loved Pierre.

"Bien sûr," Clémence said. "Of course I'll come over."

Rose's parents were divorced. Her mother kept

the house in Romainville after the split, and her father lived in central Paris for a while before he relocated to Berlin for work. His—Rose's—lovely apartment in Saint-Germain-des-Prés was not huge, but it was only steps away from the Luxembourg Gardens, Clémence's favorite park in Paris. If Clémence wasn't housesitting for her parents in the 16th, she would've looked into renting a studio apartment of her own in the 6th arrondissement.

Rose's building was off in a small alley away from the tourists, in an old, narrow building with no elevators. She lived on the fourth floor, and the girls had to carry their heavy weekend carryalls up the stairs by themselves. By the time they reached the apartment door, they needed another drink.

"*Chéri?*" Rose called when she opened the door. "Pierre, are you home?"

There was no response. The apartment had a stuffy smell to it that made Clémence think that perhaps Pierre hadn't been home at all the entire weekend.

"He's gone, isn't he?" Rose stormed into the bedroom, and Clémence followed her. She opened the closet, but all of Pierre's clothes were still there. "Oh. Maybe he has just stepped out. Ugh. I'm so crazy."

"Come on. Let's have that drink that you promised me."

But when they stepped into the kitchen, Rose screamed. "Pierre? *Mon dieu!*"

The Frenchman was sitting in a chair, but his face was down on the table—smashed onto a plate, to be exact.

"Oh lord, is he conscious?" Clémence wondered out loud. She was reluctant to approach him, but considering how distraught Rose was and how she should've been used to being around dead bodies by now, she took a few steps forward and cleared her throat. With hesitation, she tapped him on the shoulder.

"Pierre?"

"I hope he's just sleeping!" Rose exclaimed.

Clémence somehow doubted this. She touched his neck. His skin felt cold. When she felt for a pulse, there was nothing.

"I'm sorry, Rose. I think Pierre is dead."

CHAPTER TWO

*R*ose leaned back against the wall and began to hyperventilate as Clémence called the police. When she hung up, she took Rose out into the hallway. She wanted to say something comforting, but she was at a loss for words. What could you say to a friend whose boyfriend's dead body had just been found in the apartment that they shared?

Rose slumped down to the floor and buried her face in her palms. Clémence let her cry, putting an arm around her to comfort her. After a few minutes, Clémence decided that she would go back into the kitchen for clues before the police came.

There was no blood on Pierre that she could see. It could've been a medical condition. Sudden death did happen to young people. He could've had a heart defect, for example. Since he was wearing a gray T-shirt and pajama bottoms, and he'd been eating what looked like breakfast, he was probably starting his day before he fell dead somehow.

On the plate, where his head rested, were three pieces of buttered baguette bread. The rest of the baguette was beside the plate, still in the long and fitted paper bag that it came in.

Clémence sighed. The bag was lavender, with the company logo embossed on it in gold; the baguette came from Damour. Not again.

There was a Damour in Saint-Germain-des-Prés, which was smaller than the location in the 16th, but it was popular, nonetheless. As nice as it was that Pierre was loyal to her family's company to buy his baguettes from their store, this was the third death that Clémence had encountered that involved a product from Damour. If that insolent Inspector St. Clair was on this case again, he would harass her to no end about this coincidence.

What could she do? She couldn't get rid of the baguette and mess with the evidence. But she couldn't resist the urge to feel the baguette. She had already touched the dead body anyway.

The baguette felt as hard as a baseball bat.

Clémence had eaten Damour baguettes for most of her life. She knew exactly how long they lasted before they hardened. From the state of the baguette on the table, she knew that it meant Pierre had been dead since Saturday morning.

However, she still couldn't let go of the idea that there had been foul play. She looked around the rest of the apartment. Everything looked fairly normal. The TV and stereo were still in the living room. The valuable art was still on the walls, and Rose's designer clothes and purses were untouched in the closet. There didn't appear to be any signs of a break-in on the locks of the front door.

To be sure, she asked Rose, "Do you have anything valuable here that could be missing?"

Rose looked up at her with tear-stained eyes. All that relaxation at the spa had been undone in a matter of minutes.

"I-I don't think so. I have some jewelry on my dresser. It's in a box. Why? Do you think someone robbed us and then killed him?"

Her lips trembled as she spoke, and Clémence kneeled down in front of her.

"It doesn't look like it, but I just want to make sure before the police gets here."

"Is this really happening?" Rose whispered.

"You're in shock." Clémence hugged her. "I'm so sorry this happened. Do you want me to call your parents?"

"No. I can't talk to anyone right now."

Clémence nodded. "I understand. You're more than welcome to stay with me tonight."

She checked the jewelry box in Rose's room. It was full, and it didn't look as if it had been touched, either. She would've asked Rose to check the rest of the apartment if her friend wasn't in such a state of emotional shock.

It was the police's job to do the investigating, anyhow, no matter how incompetent they were at it. Clémence wasn't sure that it was a murder yet. It was unfortunate that Pierre had died, but there was nothing she could do for him now. She just wanted to know why, and only an autopsy would tell them.

Ten minutes after the police arrived, so did the hawk-nosed Cyril St. Clair. Clémence braced herself for St. Clair's snide remarks. Sure enough, he noted the baguette bag as soon as he set foot in the kitchen.

"When there's a murder, there's the color lavender," he said. "Does everybody eat something from Damour before they die?"

"Excuse me, but it's my friend's boyfriend who just died. She might hear you from the hallway, so I ask that you remain professional."

"*Pardon, madame,*" Cyril said dryly. "What's your friend's name? Was she the pitiable girl slumped in the hallway? Let's go talk to her."

"*Elle s'appelle Rose,*" Clémence said. "Be gentle with her."

Rose shook Cyril's hand feebly when he introduced himself, but she didn't get up from her spot on the floor.

"You said that you found him like this?" Cyril asked.

"Yes," Rose said slowly. "We didn't know whether he was asleep or what, so Clémence checked his pulse."

Cyril glared at Clémence. "So you touched him?"

"I had to," Clémence said. "To know what was wrong with him."

Cyril sighed. "*La heiress*, always messing with my investigations. You and that little dog of yours."

Clémence turned red. Anger was a reflex with Cyril. For Rose's sake, she swallowed all the biting insults on the tip of her tongue and took a few deep breaths instead.

"Look," she said. "We found Pierre dead, and we don't know why. As far as I can tell, he died of natural causes."

Pierre sneered. "How do I know you didn't have anything to do with this? He was eating a baguette from your store before he died. How would I know it's not another incident, like with those pistachio éclairs of yours? I wouldn't be surprised if the baguette was poisoned this time, too."

Clémence rolled her eyes. She couldn't hold her hostility back any longer. "Are you still bitter that I was the one to solve the last murder case? I'm sorry that an amateur like me could crack something faster than you could, with your hundred years of experience."

"Hardly, Damour. You just got lucky. And isn't it a coincidence that you are always the one finding the dead bodies? Maybe you're cursed, and so is your little patisserie."

"Maybe you're cursed with the inability to do your job," Clémence shot back.

She must've sounded angry enough to kill because Rose stood up and came between them.

"*Ça suffit!*" she exclaimed. "That's really enough." She turned to Cyril. "My friend had nothing to do with this. We were in Switzerland all weekend, and we can prove it with plane tickets, receipts, and credit card charges. We came home this evening to find Pierre dead. Everybody buys things from Damour, so you can stop insinuating that Clémence was involved. Now the love of my life is dead, and I want answers! If you could just stop picking on my friend, do your job, and find out what happened, I would really appreciate it."

Cyril was taken aback. It took a second for him to recompose himself. "We'll do what we can, of course," he replied haughtily.

"Clémence said that it didn't seem like anybody had broken in or taken anything," Rose continued, poking her head into the apartment. "It doesn't seem that way to me, either."

"You should know that he's been dead since Saturday," said Clémence.

"And how do you know that?" Cyril asked.

"The hardness of the baguette. Plus, Rose was here with him Friday evening before she left. She left the apartment at around seven thirty p.m.—right, Rose?"

"Right," said Rose. "Because Clémence picked me up in a taxi at that time. Pierre must've bought the baguette early Saturday morning."

"No, I doubt that," Clémence said. "He's wearing his pajamas. He bought it at night. He wouldn't go out in the morning in his pajamas."

"Hmm, you're right."

"He might've bought one of the last baguettes Friday evening. The Damour in this neighborhood closes a little earlier, at eight forty-five p.m., since this one has no *salon de thé*, but rather a small café."

"Well, thank you, ladies, for the valuable information," Cyril said sarcastically. "Now I know who to ask if I ever need to know Damour's store hours or how long one of your baguettes lasts."

"N'importe quoi," Clémence muttered. "Whatever. If you're going to continue to be rude, we're leaving. You have all the information. Just inform us when you find out what happened to him."

Something dawned on Rose. "Oh god, we have to inform Pierre's family, don't we?"

"Yes," said Cyril.

"I can't talk to them about this," she said, slumping back against the wall again.

"We'll call them, of course," a kind-looking police officer piped up. "Give us their names and numbers."

Rose reached for the phone in her purse and did as she was asked. "They're in Sydney, Australia, right now. I'm not sure if their cell phones are working there."

"Come on, Rose," said Clémence. "Let's go to my place."

"I need to gather some of my things," Rose said.

"No," said Cyril. "Nothing else gets touched. This is still a murder investigation."

"Fine," Clémence said. "I can lend you some things, Rose."

"I have some clothes in my carryall," Rose muttered.

"Let's just go." Clémence led the way down the hall.

CHAPTER THREE

*C*lémence was living in her parent's luxurious apartment in the 16th arrondissement, only steps away from the Damour flagship patisserie at 4 Place de Trocadero. Her parents were away in Asia for months, possibly up to a year, and she was there to dog-sit Miffy and keep tabs on all the stores in Paris to make sure that everything was running smoothly.

The apartment took up the entire fifth floor of the building. It had three bedrooms: her parents' main bedroom and two guest rooms. Clémence had an older brother and sister who lived in other cities. They hadn't lived in this apartment when they were growing up, but rather a humble house in Romainville, which was why the two rooms weren't personalized with any of their childhood belongings.

Clémence had taken over one of the guest bedrooms —the one connected to the spacious bathroom where she frequently took bubble baths. Her bathroom was her sanitary, and it had blue, green, and gold tiles that made her feel as if she was on vacation in Morocco.

She offered the other guest room to Rose. It was not connected to a bathroom, but it was bigger, with pale blue wallpaper and a faux fireplace. With its tall windows draped with opulent green and pink satin curtains and a small chandelier hanging from the ceiling, Clémence was sure that Rose would be comfortable there.

When Clémence got up early Monday morning, Rose was still sleeping. The night before, she had helped Rose call the boss at her PR company to explain why Rose needed to take the week off.

As Rose slept, Clémence thought she could make a quick trip to Berenice's house to pick up Miffy. Miffy was a happy Highland terrier who would cheer Rose up, at least a little bit.

Clémence would've asked the Dubois family on the third floor to dog-sit since they had done so in the past, but she hadn't wanted to because she wasn't speaking to the family's eldest son, Arthur. She didn't know whether she hated Arthur or liked him. He dated a different girl every week, and she didn't want to fall into his trap. Lately she'd been trying her best to avoid him, but it was hard since they lived in the same building. At least she hadn't run into him lately with one of his floozy girls-of-the-week like she used to.

As she took the elevator down, she hoped Arthur wouldn't come in like he did the day before she left for Switzerland. The elevator was so small that their bodies had no choice but to touch. Their arms pressed into each other, and she felt the heat of the awkward tension between them.

Arthur had been staring at the side of her face— at least she thought he did, although when she turned to him, he'd looked down at his watch, commenting that he was late. When the elevator door opened, he ran out and said good-bye. It was strange. She didn't want to see him, but when he was the one running away, she didn't want to see him go, either.

Clémence shook her head, as if wanting to shake away the whole existence of Arthur Dubois. This time, she made it down to the ground floor without seeing him, and she was relieved. She walked out the building and as fast as she could to Métro Trocadero. She would've taken a taxi, but traffic during morning rush hour in the heart of the city was usually terrible. While the Métro was also packed, at least it was faster.

Berenice Soulier lived in the 2nd arrondissement

with her parents. She was Sebastien's younger sister, and she also worked at Damour as a baker. She usually had Mondays off and had texted Clémence that she could come whenever she wanted that morning.

The apartment was near Métro Opera and a two-minute walk from the Palais Garner, the gorgeous opera house that inspired *The Phantom of the Opera*. Clémence walked down Boulevard des Italians and turned on Rue de la Michodiere to Berenice's building. The Souliers lived on the sixth floor. They had even bought out the chambres de bonne, the servant rooms on the top floor, and converted them into a second floor for their apartment. When Clémence came out of the elevator, Berenice was already waiting for her at the door with Miffy in her arms.

The girls greeted each other with *bisous*. Clémence took Miffy into her arms and kissed her, as well. Berenice showed her in. Clémence had been to her home before. Her parents were lovely, but both of them had already left for work, so the girls had the apartment to themselves. Clémence was glad because she wanted to tell Berenice right away about what had happened.

"You look so refreshed!" Berenice said. "If I didn't have to go to my cousin's wedding on Saturday, I totally would've gone to Switzerland with you guys. How was it?"

"Zurich was amazing," said Clémence. "And so was the hotel, but our getaway feels like such a long time ago. So much has happened."

She told Berenice about Pierre.

"No way!" she exclaimed. "Another dead body?"

"You're telling me. Can't I go a month without finding one of them?"

"Poor Rose. How is she?"

"I'm not sure. She's probably in shock."

"Do you think she'll want some company today?"

"Maybe. She gets bored without social interaction, and I'm sure she'd appreciate the distraction. I was counting on Miffy to cheer her up, but if you're free, I'm sure she'd like your company, as well."

"Of course I'll come. I didn't have plans today except to lounge around and watch trashy soaps. You know, I don't think I've ever even met Pierre before."

"I've met him a couple of times," said Clémence. "But usually when I'm at Rose's house. He wasn't that social. Rose said he had a tiny circle of friends he stuck with and didn't have any interest to meet new people."

"I wonder what happened to him."

Clémence shrugged. "Beats me. I just hope we get some answers soon. Maybe Rose feels some guilt.

They had been fighting before she left, and it was why she wanted to get away for the weekend."

"Oh no. Maybe she feels like she could've prevented his death if she didn't leave."

"Let's get going." Clémence put on Miffy's leash. "I left Rose a note, but I don't want to leave her alone for too long."

Berenice grabbed her purse. "*On y va.* Should we pick up something for breakfast? I was munching on a baguette, ironically enough, but I'm still hungry."

"The baguette's not from Damour, I hope."

"No, the *boulangerie* downstairs."

"I'd pick up something from Damour on the way home," said Clémence, "but I wonder if it'll upset Rose."

"We can always remove the packaging."

As the girls and Miffy headed towards the Métro, Clémence's phone rang.

"It's St. Clair." Clémence answered eagerly, hoping he had the answers they were waiting for.

"Brain hemorrhage," Cyril boomed into the phone. "Due to blunt impact. Pierre Colombier was killed."

Clémence stopped in her tracks so suddenly that Miffy was pulled back by the leash. "What? *Mais non!*"

"Si. I tried calling your friend—what's her name? The victim's girlfriend?"

"Rose Viard."

"Right, but she's not picking up. I have questions. Is she home?"

"I suppose," said Clémence. "She was sleeping, the last I checked, but I'm not at my house with her at the moment."

"You can tell her the news, then."

"Are you sure it was murder?"

"I wasn't the one doing the test," Cyril said. "Now that you know that it is murder, stay out of my case. All right, Damour?"

Cyril hung up.

"What is it?" Berenice asked.

Clémence took a deep breath.

"Well, Pierre was murdered, after all."

CHAPTER FOUR

*C*lémence and Berenice broke the news to Rose after she had time to digest her breakfast.

"Murdered? Are you sure?" Rose's eyes were as wide as saucers. "Who would kill Pierre?"

"No clue," said Clémence. "Do you have any ideas?"

"I—I don't know."

"I know it's hard, sweetie," said Berenice, "but can you tell us a bit more about him?"

Rose slumped down on the red leather couch in the salon. She put her hands over her face and breathed in deeply. Clémence and Berenice looked at each other, wondering if Rose was going to start crying. She surprised them by sitting upright and taking a sip of her espresso that sat on the glass coffee table.

"I met Pierre when I was in school finishing my MBA," she started. "I thought he was a bit serious at first, but the more we got to know each other, the more comfortable we became. When we decided to be exclusive, we were inseparable; I was over the moon in love with him. I mean, he's well-educated, he's from an upper-class family, we both have ambitious career goals, and he could be very romantic and attentive—well, for the first few months that we knew each other, anyway.

"He moved in with me a year ago, and that was when we started fighting more. It was around the same time that he got his project management job at F.R. Fraser, so I thought it was because he was overworked and stressed all the time. God, is it too early for some wine?"

Clémence jumped up. "It's never too early for wine."

In the kitchen, she uncorked a bottle of red. Berenice helped her take the wine glasses back in to the salon.

Rose took a sip. Then she chugged the whole glass. "Thanks. I needed that."

"Did Pierre have any enemies?"

"Sometimes he would complain about his coworkers. I think there's one coworker that he always complained about, Paolo something, who was his main competition. Paolo Bruno. Pierre is a competitive guy. He always needed to be at the top of the class when we were in school. I don't think he would've dated me if I had better grades than he did, because he would've resented it. He resented anyone who was remotely better in anything, or who had the potential to surpass him. Oh, and he also complained about his assistant all the time, saying she was inefficient and lazy. Her name is Mary, I think. That's all I know."

"That's helpful," said Clémence. "What about his friends?"

"He only has two friends that he hangs out with all the time, Adam and Thierry. He's known them forever, and they hang around the apartment sometimes, but they're definitely not killers. Gosh, I really don't know who would hate him enough to kill him."

"And who would break in?" Berenice asked. "The attack must've been a surprise to him if he was just sitting at the breakfast table, minding his own business."

"Poor Pierre." Rose withered back into the couch again.

"They could've only gotten in through the front door," said Clémence. "The windows didn't look tampered with, and they were locked from the inside. The exterior of the building is completely flat, so it wouldn't be an easy feat to go through the window when there's nothing to latch onto on the walls, unless it was a ninja or something."

"What about the front door?" Berenice asked. "Was that tampered with?"

"I don't think so," said Clémence. "I do have to lock this apartment and put on the alarm whenever I go out. Our insurance company requires us to. Since it's such a big apartment in an expensive neighborhood, I lock the door from the inside when I come home, but Rose's apartment is quite small. You probably don't lock it from the inside when you are home, right? Even at night?"

"No," said Rose. "We don't. Our neighborhood is safe, and I suppose there are way bigger and more luxurious apartments in the neighborhood to steal from. Pierre and I only lock the doors from the outside when nobody is home."

"So the killer might've found a way to open the door. If you didn't lock the door with a key from the outside or the inside, it's possible to break in by taking, say, a thin sheet of plastic and sliding it between the door and the wall to unlock it."

"How do you know so much about breaking in?" Berenice asked.

"I was locked out of my old apartment once," said Clémence. "Back when I lived with Mathieu in the Marais. He was in class for three hours and wouldn't answer the phone, so I had to ask my neighbor for help. She gave me an old X-ray sheet from her health file, and it actually worked."

"That's pretty brilliant," said Berenice.

"Yes, so unfortunately, it's not too hard to break into a house. It's just strange because this killer didn't steal anything. I think the main motive must've been to get Pierre. Now the question is why?"

"And who?" said Rose.

"You know, someone could've had a key," said Berenice.

"True," said Clémence. "Who else would have an extra key to the apartment, Rose?"

"Just me and Pierre. It's my father's apartment, so he has a key as well." Rose jerked her head up toward Clémence with a startled expression. "But there's no way my father had anything to do with this. He lives in Berlin, anyway."

Clémence nodded. "Of course he wouldn't." Although the idea had crossed Clémence's mind. Anything was possible.

"Besides, my father likes Pierre. He even wants him to propose. Both my parents do."

"We just need to focus on the people who don't

like Pierre," said Clémence. "And find out why. We ought to start with this Paolo guy. What exactly did Pierre used to say about him?"

Rose refilled her wine glass and took another long sip. "Just a bunch of insults. He'd say that Paolo was an arrogant imbecile who didn't know his ass from his elbow. Paolo is probably just a really smart guy. You have to be, to work at F.R. Fraser. The company only hires the best. Paolo probably also rubs him the wrong way because he's friendly. In fact, Pierre often complains about how much he smiles at work, and how talkative and upbeat he is."

"Leave it to a Frenchman to find smiles irritating," said Berenice.

"Paolo is Italian," said Rose. "So he probably doesn't fully understand how serious the work atmosphere is here. I haven't met him, though, because Pierre doesn't like going to company holiday parties, and he never socializes with his coworkers outside of work. I doubt he even has lunch with anyone. Actually, I doubt he eats lunch outside. He probably just eats at his desk."

"Wow," said Berenice. "He was that antisocial, huh?"

"He's that, and his job is also incredibly demanding. Even on holidays, he's always catching up on e-mails. There never seems to be a moment's rest with him." Rose sighed. "Seemed, I mean. I have to get used to speaking about him in the past tense, don't I? The thing about Pierre was that he was brilliant and a hard worker. He was the first person in the office and the last to leave. That's why he kept getting promoted over the others. Paolo was his main competitor at the position he was in."

"Maybe Paolo is also competitive," said Clémence.

"Yeah," said Berenice. "Maybe Paolo knew he couldn't match Pierre's level of productivity."

"I definitely want to talk to him," said Clémence.

"I suppose he's at the office," said Rose. "He should be. I'd go with you, but I don't think I can handle that, right now."

"Don't worry," said Clémence. "I'll just go. I'll tell the truth and say that I'm a friend of yours, picking up Pierre's things for you, and I'll try to run into this Paolo guy."

"Want me to go with you?" asked Berenice.

Clémence looked at Rose in her sad state. Rose was trying to keep strong, but Clémence knew that she was vulnerable and needed support in a time like this.

"Can you stay with Rose?" she asked. Then she looked at the clock. "Actually, it's almost lunchtime, and Paolo sounds like the kind of guy who would take his time enjoying his lunch. We can eat lunch together, and I'll go pay him a visit right after."

Just then, Miffy jumped up into Rose's lap and snuggled into her. Rose's sullen face crinkled into a smile as she stroked Miffy's white fur.

CHAPTER FIVE

*A*fter lunch, Clémence took a quick shower and left. She wasn't in a huge rush because she wanted to make sure that Paolo would be in the office when she got there. She had looked him up on the Internet with Rose's help. His photo on LinkedIn featured him smiling with both rows of teeth, and he was incredibly well dressed in a well-cut suit and pink silk tie. With dark hair and tanned skin, Paolo looked too relaxed to have lived in Paris for long. But did this happy-go-lucky Italian also exhibit the qualities of a killer?

As Clémence continued scrutinizing his photo and profile on her smartphone, the elevator stopped. Arthur got in before she had time to panic. Arthur was wearing a pink dress shirt with a fuchsia sweater tied around his neck.

"Bonjour," he said in his usual stiff way.

"I don't think you're wearing enough pink," Clémence couldn't help but comment. While he usually wore those pieces separately, she thought he was going overboard this time.

He looked down at his beige khakis. "You're right. I should've gone with the pink pants, as well."

Clémence nodded feebly, not knowing what to say.

He broke from his stony expression and laughed. "I'm kidding."

"Phew."

The elevator door closed. She tried to ignore his warm scent and the sudden intimacy of his arm pressing into hers in the tiny elevator.

"I shouldn't have to defend my fashion choices," Arthur said. "This is a classic look."

Straight out of the preppy handbook, Clémence thought. Instead she said, "You're right. Pink is your color. This is a free country, and you should wear whatever you want."

"Why thank you," Arthur said. "I haven't seen you around lately. Quoi de neuf?"

"What's new?" Clémence repeated. "Oh, this and that. What about you?"

She could feel his brown eyes on her. But she refused to make direct eye contact—it was a trap. No way was she going to be one of the girls who did the Sunday morning walk of shame. She knew herself well enough to know that the more she interacted with him, the more of a chance that she would succumb to him. Like many women, she was weak for men who didn't treat her as well as they could've. In order for Clémence to keep her standards high, she had to refuse the guys who weren't up to par. Unfortunately, that also meant she had a smaller pool to draw from.

Maybe she was being picky, or insecure, but she had to take protective measures for her heart. Whenever she opened up to someone, she had been disappointed, hurt, or brutally bashed. It was good to have boundaries, although lately it had felt as if those boundaries had turned into impenetrable walls.

"Moi?" Arthur said. "I've been busy."

"Hmm."

"Not that kind of busy. I mean there's an end in sight with my Ph.D., so it's been going well. Are you still seeing that American guy, what's-his-name?"

Arthur was referring to John, whom she met when she was investigating a murder case recently. She had suspected the American banker of murder and had agreed to go on a date with him to obtain information. Fortunately he wasn't the murderer, which meant she hadn't gone out with a killer. John had wanted to continue dating Clémence, but she wasn't so sure. During their date, they had run into Arthur on his own date with a blond bombshell. From the way John had drooled over the blonde, Clémence knew that he wasn't good for a long-term relationship, and she'd never returned his texts. Then she went to Switzerland for the weekend and pretty much forgot about him.

"Why so interested in my love life?" Clémence retorted. The elevator door opened, and she stepped out first.

"Just wondering," said Arthur. "He didn't seem like your type."

Clémence raised an eyebrow. "How would you know what my type is?"

"I know you better than you think I do."

She didn't know why, but the comment annoyed her. "I know why you don't like John. It's because you're just like him."

Her words vexed Arthur, from what she could read on his face.

"How? I'm nothing like him."

"Sure you are. You both are rich, overly educated, pretty cocky, and work in finance. Then again, I'm describing ninety percent of the guys around here."

"You know me less than you think you do," said Arthur.

So you don't sleep with a different girl every week?
Clémence wanted to blurt out. But she kept silent.

They walked for a few minutes without speaking.
The sun was out, and Clémence would have enjoyed
the sunshine if she wasn't self-conscious about Arthur
being by her side. Did he want to walk together, or
was this awkward for him, as well?

She walked as fast as she could, but since he was
so tall, he only needed to stroll in his leisurely way to
keep up with her.

"Are you going to the Métro?" he asked.

"Oui."

"I'm going to Métro Miromesnil."

"I'm going there, too—" Clémence said before she
stopped herself. She didn't want to be stuck on the
train with Arthur for another fifteen minutes.

"So we can take the nine line together." He
smiled.

Clémence inwardly groaned. Why did he have to
have such a nice smile? He wasn't all bad when he
smiled. His entire face lit up when he did, and
Clémence had to look away. What was the matter
with her, lately?

They made their way down to the Métro in more
silence.

When they got to the platform, Arthur turned to
her. "You know, I texted you once."

"Oh?" Clémence replied.

"Did you not get it? Last week."

Clémence had indeed received it, but she had ignored it. "No," she lied. "What did it say?"

"*'Ça va?'*"

"That's it? Just *'ça va'*?"

"Yeah."

"Why?"

Arthur gave her a funny look. "Just to say hi and see how you were doing."

"Seems kind of pointless," said Clémence. "I would've just texted back *'ça va'*. I'm really not into texting."

"That's how people communicate these days, by texting."

"Texting is for making plans, not to make small talk."

Arthur's full lips curled into a smile. A lock of his chestnut-colored hair curled down to his forehead. He looked so adorable, and Clémence resisted the urge to brush the curl away.

"But you start a conversation with small talk," he said.

"I'm just not into communicating via texting or the Internet."

Arthur cocked his head to one side and examined

her. "That's what's intriguing about you. You have no Internet presence. It's kind of cute."

Clémence blushed. "Have you been trying to find me online?"

"Well, I liked the Damour fan page on Facebook, but you're nowhere to be found anywhere."

"I'm a very private person," she said. "So stop Googling me. You'll never find me."

The train came. Although it was a Monday afternoon, the train was still crowded. It was the beginning of tourist season in Paris, and once again, Clémence was pressed too close for comfort to Arthur.

He leaned over her, and she could smell his familiar warm scent in spite of the putrid smell of a crowded Métro. She couldn't help it—she looked up at him, met his eyes, and a hot electric current passed between them.

"Your eyes are really blue," Arthur said.

His lips were close enough to touch hers. Clémence backed away, or tried to. There were too many people, and she couldn't take a step anywhere without stepping into anyone. Did she really have to stay in this position for the entire ride?

"Thanks," she muttered. "I like your, um, nose."

The truth was, Clémence liked everything about him—his dark hair and eyes, his plush lips, his full eyelashes, his cute ears, even his forehead. But the nose seemed like the most neutral feature to comment on, even though it was stupid to verbalize, as she realized the moment it came out of her mouth.

"Oh, do you?" Arthur arched an eyebrow.

She changed the subject before she turned really pink. "Where are you going, anyway? At Miromesnil?"

"I have an appointment with a consulting company. They want me to work for them part time. I'm not sure if my school schedule and workload will allow me to, but the head of the company has agreed to answer some questions I have for my Ph.D."

"Wow, that's amazing. Sounds like you're making progress."

"I am," he said proudly. "And where are you off to?"

"Oh..."

It was a long story that she wasn't sure whether she should tell Arthur. This was the third murder that she was investigating. Murders had been happening around her ever since she returned to the city. Arthur, like Inspector St. Clair, would probably think that she, or the store, was cursed. In a way, she wouldn't blame them. Why did people keep getting killed when they were munching on one of her products?

"You're more dressed up than usual," said Arthur. "You're not baiting another murder suspect, are you?"

Clémence had styled her brown hair into a sleek bob with a straightening iron. She was wearing a white blouse and a black pencil skirt with kitten heels. It was how she would've dressed if she had an office job. Since she was heading to an office, she hoped to blend in with the other employees.

"I just have an appointment somewhere."

"That's pretty vague," said Arthur.

"Like I said, I'm a private person."

When they got out and went up to street level, Clémence waved good-bye to Arthur. She still didn't know whether their hellos and good-byes required bisous, the kisses on the cheeks that were the custom between friends in France. But Arthur leaned in with his left cheek facing her, and she obliged with the bisous. Did this mean that she would have to kiss him every time they saw each other?

"Hey, uh." Arthur looked down at his shoes. He suddenly seemed nervous, for some reason. "You know those flowers that you received over a month ago?"

"You mean that big bouquet of roses?" Clémence said.

"Yes, those."

"What about them?"

"I did send them."

Clémence didn't know how to react at first. She had always suspected it, and she'd even confronted him about it, but he had vehemently denied it.

"Are you sure?" she asked. "Because you seemed really offended when I asked you whether they were from you a while back."

"I know," he said sheepishly. "I was a little stupid back then."

Clémence almost laughed. Arthur admitting that he was stupid? Maybe he was right: she didn't know Arthur as well as she thought she did.

"Well, thanks for the flowers."

"You're welcome."

They stood on the sidewalk staring at each other for an awkward moment. Arthur spoke up again.

"I bought them because I was sorry when you got attacked, but I think I was also confused about how I felt about you so I didn't want you to know." He took a deep breath. "Look, you drive me crazy sometimes. I admit, I've dated plenty of girls in the past, but I never stay interested for long. There's just something intriguing about you that I want to get to know more of. God, I hope I don't sound too corny right now."

Clémence broke into a small smile. He sounded sweet, in fact. If he could only show more of this side, she could really allow herself to fall for him.

"Anyway," he continued. "I was wondering if you wanted to go to lunch sometime."

"Lunch?"

"Yeah. It's more casual than a formal dinner and nicer than just getting a drink. Lunch."

Clémence thought about it. Was it really a good idea to date her neighbor? She had been single for a while now. Sure she'd dated while on her travels, but she always knew that she could pack for the next country and leave the dates behind. With Arthur, she couldn't pack up and leave; he lived in the same building. If things didn't work out, they were stuck.

"Can I think about it?" Clémence asked.

Arthur nodded. His face was less open, impenetrable again. She had not given the answer that he'd hoped for.

"Sure. Text me this time. Ciao."

Clémence watched him walk away and turn a corner. She reached for her smartphone and checked the address of F.R. Fraser on her map. As she followed the directions, her mother phoned her.

Her parents were still in Tokyo to oversee the first Damour patisserie in Japan. The fever of the grand store opening still hadn't died down yet. There were daily lines around the block for their macarons and other desserts and pastries. The salon de thé was booked for weeks in advance. Her mother was just

calling to update her and to ask how her trip to
Zurich was. They chatted a while longer, but
Clémence didn't want to tell her about Rose's
boyfriend's death just yet.

When she reached the building where F.R. Fraser
operated, she managed to talk the security guard into
letting her in. She simply told the truth: that she was
collecting something for an employee who had died
recently. After receiving condolences, she was allowed
in through the turnstile. The main foyer was modern,
with a man-made waterfall dribbling down a marble
wall. There was a café in one corner for employees.
She pressed the elevator button. When one of the
elevator doors opened, the presence of the man stepping out shocked her.

CHAPTER SIX

"You? Again?" Clémence shook her head in disbelief.

"Can't stay away from me for long, can you?" Arthur stepped out, grinning in all his pink glory.

"What are you doing here?"

"The guy I had a meeting with at Mable & Best is still out for lunch, so I thought I'd take a walk. So your appointment is here, as well?"

Clémence couldn't believe they had both ended up in the same building. Paris was really like a small town sometimes. She figured she might as well tell him.

"Okay, I'm going to F.R. Fraser," she admitted. "The financial firm."

"Of course I know what F.R. Fraser is."

"I have to collect the things for my friend's boyfriend who works there. Or used to work there, rather. He was murdered." She filled him in on everything.

Arthur shook his head in shock. "But you're not just here to collect his things, are you?"

"Yes I am," she replied.

"No, you're dressed up. You're up to something. Who do you suspect is the murderer, this time? Spill it."

Clémence sighed. Must Arthur get involved every time?

"Fine." She briefed him on Pierre's coworker, and how she wanted to interrogate him.

"How are you going to do that without making it sound like you're accusing him of murder?"

"I have ways."

Arthur gave her a hard look. "You haven't even prepared what you're going to say, have you?"

"I took improv classes in *lycée*. I'm good at thinking on my feet. You know, feel my way into it. It's worked so far."

"Maybe you need someone with experience in the finance world to help you." Arthur's chest seemed to inflate by the second.

Clémence snorted. "If you mean someone who

sleeps in till ten every morning and plays tennis, sure."

Arthur expressed mock outrage. "I don't think you have a clue as to the breadth of the talents that I possess."

"Please don't make me roll my eyes." Clémence got into the elevator and pressed the button for the second floor. Arthur got in after her. "I'm not sure if it's a good idea for you to come, Arthur. I'm trying to be inconspicuous here, and all that pink might cause a commotion."

"Damour, let a real man get some answers out of this suspect. What's his name?"

"Paolo. Paolo Bruno."

When they got out of the elevator, they could see through the glass wall into the office of F.R. Fraser. It was a busy environment, with people on headsets working with multiple computer screens. The receptionist was fielding numerous calls.

"They're not going to even notice us," said Arthur. "Come on. Let's go."

"Oh, fine."

They pushed through the glass door. Sure enough, the secretary was too busy speaking on the phone to even look up.

"Rose said that Pierre's desk is at the corner on the right side of the room." Clémence led the way.

His desk was already bare. There were no picture frames or knickknacks like the other employees had on their desks. He only had a bunch of pens in a cup and a calculator lying out, as well as a couple of finance books and a laptop cord, but no laptop. In his drawers were some single-wrapped madeleines and a beige stapler.

"Did somebody already come to clean the desk out?" Arthur asked.

"Rose did say that he was a very minimalistic guy."

"What about his computer?"

"He probably took it home with him. I remember seeing a laptop on the table in his bedroom. The police probably took it, though."

"It would help to go through his e-mails," said Arthur.

"I hope they do find something," said Clémence. "Although I just don't know with St. Clair."

"He's an idiot," Arthur said.

"Ain't that the truth."

"So where's this Paolo guy?"

Clémence shushed him.

"Relax," said Arthur. "Everyone's involved with their headsets and computers. We don't even exist to them."

Just then Clémence noticed the lanky figure of

Inspector Cyril St. Clair. He was going into one of the offices on the opposite side of the room. He didn't seem to have noticed Clémence, and she was relieved, because he would've probably caused a scene, trying to kick her out and prevent her from investigating.

"He must be interrogating the boss," said Clémence. "Come on."

Nobody glanced their way as they walked across the room to the big offices where the walls and doors were also made of glass. Everybody seemed to put on an illusion of privacy, especially when everything was on display for all to see. Clémence picked up some papers from a recycling bin on the way to the office that she'd seen Cyril enter. The paper she would simply hold in her hand. She planned on standing close with Arthur. In the event that anyone walked past them, they could pretend to be discussing something work related in the documents.

It was a very stressful work environment. Phones were ringing, numerous voices were chatting away at once, and there was the gurgling sound of the espresso machine coming from the break room. Everybody was hyped up on caffeine. Since the office door was made out of glass, she couldn't stand in front of it to eavesdrop; it was too difficult to make out what Cyril and the boss were saying.

"I don't think the people here got the memo about Pierre's death yet," Clémence said to Arthur.

"Maybe they did, and they just don't care."

"No, St. Clair's probably just breaking the news now. It's only a matter of time before word gets out. We have to find Paolo and find out what we can before St. Clair tries to interrogate him."

Clémence looked carefully at every employee. There must've been over fifty people. Then finally, she spotted Paolo, walking in their direction. He wore a gray Italian cut suit, a white dress shirt, and an electric blue tie; he was by far the best-dressed man in the office. He was a lot more fit in person than he had appeared on LinkedIn. His build suggested that he spent some time in the gym.

"That's him," Clémence whispered.

"Who? Paolo?" Arthur spun around so suddenly that he caught Paolo's attention. Clémence sighed. Why did Arthur have to be so obvious about it?

"Bonjour," Paolo greeted them. He was all square white teeth. "Are you two new? I haven't seen you in the office before. I'm Paolo."

"Je suis," uh, Edouard," Arthur said, shaking his offered hand. Paolo's gaze lingered on him a second longer before he shook Clémence's hand. She introduced herself as Juliette.

"We don't work here," said Clémence. "We're

actually friends of Pierre's. Pierre Colombier—do you know him?"

"Yes, I know him. Is anything the matter with him? It's not like him to miss work."

He was looking at Arthur even when she was the one talking.

"He's ill," said Arthur.

"He must be severely ill," said Paolo. "I've seen him come into work when he was sick. Is everything okay?"

"Fine," Clémence lied. "He's just getting over the flu."

"The flu? In late spring? That's bad luck."

"Yes." Arthur nodded. "We work close by, and we just wanted to pick up a few things for Pierre so he can work from his bed."

Paolo nodded and laughed. "Classic Pierre. He works even when he's dying."

Clémence and Arthur managed to laugh back. If Paolo only knew.

"What could you possibly pick up?" Paolo asked. "The guy's so secretive that he always takes home everything he brings."

"Pierre mentioned something about, uh, the documents from the latest project that he's working on?" Clémence said.

"Ah, you mean the Madison project. We were

supposed to work on it together, but Pierre threw a fit as usual and demanded we both go our own ways to tackle it separately. Don't tell me he wants to see what I have so soon."

"He does," said Clémence. "You know Pierre."

"Believe me, I do."

Paolo led them to his desk—which, in contrast to Pierre's, was a tornado of a mess. Despite the thick files, the binders, and books all in chaotic piles, he was somehow able to find what he was looking for rather quickly.

"Here. It's a draft of what I have so far. Pierre can tell me what he thinks." He cringed. "Or maybe I should give him a call—you know, to be courteous."

"No," Arthur cut in. "He's not taking calls at the moment."

"Phew," said Pierre. "I mean, I'm sorry he's sick, but he's a little high strung, you know? Not exactly someone you want to spend time on the phone with because he'll basically bark orders at you."

He chuckled again, and Clémence joined in.

"We're friends of his, so we don't know what he's like at work," she said.

"Oh, I'm his coworker, so I don't know what he's like as a friend," Paolo joked. "He's a bit hard to get to know. Maybe it's just the French work environment. How do you know him again?"

"My friend Rose is his girlfriend."

"Ah, so you're not really a friend of Pierre's."

"Honestly, we don't know him that well, either," Clémence admitted.

"Is it different here from the Italian work environment?" Arthur asked.

"Yes, you can tell by my accent that I'm Italian?" Paolo eyed Arthur flirtatiously. "I guess it's quite strong. In Italy, it's not so competitive that coworkers are openly hostile. Maybe 'hostile' is a strong word. I think Pierre is the type to get his own way, and nobody else can get in his way. At the same time, I do kind of admire him, because it's taken him far in such a short amount of time."

"I heard he's up for a promotion to be your boss," said Clémence.

"It's a high possibility." Paolo was still making eyes at Arthur and moving in on him. Arthur leaned back against the glass wall. "Honestly, I know he's your friend, but I would probably transfer if that were to happen. It's hard enough being his coworker. It's unfortunate that he's so hard to work with, because he sure is a looker."

Paolo gave Arthur a wink. Arthur pressed his lips together and turned to Clémence. She'd never seen him look so uncomfortable.

"Yes, he's quite handsome, isn't he?" Clémence

couldn't suppress a smile. "So who else finds Pierre to be a pain in the ass in this office? Or are there people who actually like him?"

"Pierre's a bit of a Hitler around here," Paolo said. "We don't take it personally. That's just his personality. Maybe it would be a different story if we were to get to know him outside of work."

"I do think Pierre can be quite antisocial," Clémence agreed.

"We're his minions, really. I feel sorry for Mary, his assistant. She gets it the worst."

"Who is Mary, anyway?"

Paolo looked around. His gaze followed a petite bored-looking brunette who was walking toward the office where St. Clair was currently in. Clémence wondered if she was going to be called in and questioned about the murder. They didn't have much time before the news of Pierre's murder spread.

"That's her?" Clémence asked.

"Yes," said Paolo. "But it looks like she's busy. She just went into our boss's office."

"Well, we better go," Arthur said. "We got what we came for. Thanks."

"Anytime." Paolo gave him a sly smile. "It was lovely meeting you."

As Clémence exited through the glass door and Arthur followed, Paolo called after them.

"Wait. Edouard? Can I speak to you for just a minute?"

"Moi?" Arthur looked flustered. "Um, sure."

"I'll wait for you in the hall." Clémence grinned.

She wondered what Paolo would say, but she had a pretty good idea.

CHAPTER SEVEN

When Arthur came out of the office, his face was as pink as his shirt. "So what did he want?" Clémence asked with a sly smile.

He quickly pressed the elevator button a few times with force.

"He wanted to have dinner," Arthur muttered.

Clémence laughed. "He asked you out? I knew it! What did you say?"

"I turned him down, of course! Why would he think I'm gay?"

Clémence raised an eyebrow and eyed the fuchsia sweater tied around his pink shirt.

"Studies have proved that men who wear pink are more confident," he said. "That guy must not know that only men of a certain class can pull off pink."

"Really, you should be flattered. A good-looking guy like that?"

Arthur snapped his head toward her. "You think he's good looking?"

"He's not bad. Too bad he swings for your team."

Arthur groaned. "When we go out for lunch, you're paying."

"Hey, who said I agreed to go out to lunch with you?"

"After this, you really owe me, Damour."

"You brought this on yourself." Clémence laughed. "I didn't even want you to come in the first place. But at least we got some information. Paolo doesn't seem to be involved, don't you think?"

"I doubt it, too."

"I have to admit that it did help for you to be there, since he was so friendly and open with you. I do wish I had spoken to Mary. We might have to come back."

"We?" Arthur exclaimed. "I'm never coming back here again."

"And you were so enthused about helping me with the case earlier."

"You're on your own, doll."

When they got into the elevator alone together, again, Clémence started giggling at the whole situation. "You really made my day, Arthur."

"Laugh now, Damour, but you'll pay at lunch."

"If you really want a free meal, I'm sure Paolo would be more than happy to take you."

Arthur pinched Clémence on the arm. "It's true though. If I were gay, I'd attract the hottest men. How could you say no to lunch with a guy like me?"

Clémence raised an eyebrow at him. She gave him a once-over and pretended to consider it. "Persistence pays off, Dubois. Fine, I'll go to lunch with you. Just lunch."

She figured she'd give him a chance. When Arthur was uncomfortable, she thought he was kind of cute. Maybe she had a sadistic streak, because she loved to see him squirm.

"What kind of food do you like?" he asked. "Do you like sushi?"

"Love it," said Clémence.

"Great. I'll text you when I find a good restaurant."

Arthur went to the fourth floor for his meeting. When she took the Métro home, she couldn't stop thinking about him. And she started to worry about their lunch date. Did she really agree to date Arthur? He claimed that he stopped serial dating, but could she really trust him? Could she really trust herself?

If this was going to work, she would have to place some boundaries, some old-fashioned rules. For one, she would not jump into bed with him. Not until he told her that he loved her—and she had ways of telling if a guy really meant it or not. She wanted to get to know him better first, and that would take time. She doubted that he ever tried to get to know his former girlfriends before he slept with them.

Did she and Arthur even have anything in common? She knew nothing about macroeconomics, and he didn't know much about patisseries and painting except, like everybody else in France, that he liked to eat pastries and go to museums every so often.

They shared a few misadventures in crime solving —that seemed to be their common bond. When the murders stopped, then what?

Clémence couldn't believe she'd worked herself into this type of obsessive thinking again. It was just lunch. And she should really be focusing all her attention on Pierre's murder. St. Clair seemed to have a grip on the situation; he thought in the same vein as she had, questioning his coworkers first. She wondered what he thought of Mary, and what Mary had to say about Pierre.

When she got home, Berenice had been replaced by Rose's mother Diane.

"*Bonjour*, Clémence." Diane gave Clémence bisous on the cheeks.

Diane smelled like Dior perfume, her signature scent. She looked like the older version of her daughter. Both women had big brown eyes and dirty blond hair. Diane's hair was cut in a cool shaggy do, but unfortunately she had gone the Californian housewife route of injecting her lips with fillers. Clémence thought she'd looked better before, but she didn't want to judge. Some women needed to do something in order to feel attractive as they got older.

"When I called Rose this morning, she told me everything, and I took the taxi straight over. I hope you don't mind."

"Of course not. I'm glad you're here. Where is Berenice?"

"She got called into work. Rose had a stomachache after lunch, and she's napping to sleep it off. I want her to stay in Romainville with me, but she seems adamant about staying in Paris for the time being. She says you're helping the police investigate who really killed Pierre?"

"I am," Clémence confirmed, "but I don't know if it's the best thing for Rose to stay here. Maybe it would be better for her to go to Romainville so she can grieve."

"I know. I've told her, but she wouldn't go, and I don't want to leave her alone. I mean, what a terrible ordeal. Pierre murdered? Good heavens."

"You're welcome to stay," said Clémence. "There's plenty of room."

"You don't mind?"

"Of course not."

"I promise not to be a bother. In fact, I'll cook for you girls. It doesn't seem like you have much in the fridge at the moment."

Clémence laughed. "Usually I'll just eat at my store, or I grab something quick on my way home."

"Rose is the same. Girls of this generation, these days. Too busy to cook, but I don't blame ya. Being a working girl is something to be proud of."

"Thanks, and I do appreciate a good home-cooked meal. I've missed eating some of your famous dishes. My favorite is your pâté aux pommes de terre."

"That's everybody's favorite," she said. "And funnily enough, it's what I want to make for dinner. About Pierre, have you found anything so far?"

Clémence told her about how she tried to talk to his coworker, but he was now off her suspect list.

"Are you sure it's still not possible that it's him?" Diane asked. "The workplace is so competitive these days. People all backstabbing each other. It's all fear from the financial crisis and people losing their jobs. I wouldn't be surprised if somebody would want to get rid of a brilliant guy like Pierre from the competition."

"Enough to murder him in his home?"

Diane sighed and shook her head. "Who's to say what motivates people, these days?"

"Have you met Pierre?"

"Sure. Rose brought him home on several occasions."

"What did you think of him?"

Diane thought about it. Clémence could tell that she was trying to choose her words carefully. "He seemed a bit, well, quiet. I didn't really see what Rose saw in him at first. He had no sense of humor, just like my ex-husband."

Diane gave a shrill laugh. Clémence knew that her divorce had been a sore point. Rose's father had run off with a woman half his age, whom he had met at work. He and Diane had divorced six years ago, and Diane kept the house in Romainville.

"But he seems like a nice guy. Very ambitious. What about you? What did you think about him? No need to mince words."

"I don't know. He did seem like a nice enough guy, but I agree that he was a bit humorless."

"You know how girls can be. They're attracted to men like their fathers."

"Is that so?" Clémence said.

"That's what they say. Freud, at least. Rose's father was just as humorless."

"And you believe that?"

"Maybe. Or at least some version of their fathers."

"I don't know about that theory," said Clémence. "My father's the greatest guy I know, but I keep dating these arrogant jerks."

Diane laughed. "What, so you're in love with a jerk right now?"

Clémence squirmed. "I wouldn't say in love. We haven't even gone on a date yet."

"Oh, but you will?"

She nodded. "Yes, this week."

Clémence broke into a smile. It felt good to confide in someone. She was used to telling her mom about the guys she dated, but it would be strange to when it came to Arthur, because her mom knew Arthur's mom, and they were all neighbors. Clémence also didn't want to discuss it with her friends yet, since she'd told them how much she despised Arthur.

"To be young and in love." Diane sighed dreamily.

CHAPTER EIGHT

"*S*ebastien is acting so weird," Berenice said. "He called me to fill in for him this afternoon, but he won't tell me what he's up to."

"Any guesses?" Clémence asked.

They were in the kitchen, where Berenice was preparing croissants to be baked. Clémence had dropped in after receiving a text from Berenice informing her where she had disappeared off to.

"I think it has something to do with where he goes off to on Tuesday and Thursday evenings," Berenice said. "I'm tempted to follow him, one of these days."

"He'll probably never speak to you again if you do," Clémence said.

"Sure he would. We're family. He knows what I'm capable of. But I'll find out what he's up to one of these days. The truth always comes out, sooner or later. So what are you going to do next for Pierre's case?"

"I'm not sure," said Clémence. "I was going to talk to the assistant, but Cyril beat me to it. I do want to talk to her, but I wonder if Cyril already found something. I hope he does."

"Rose was sobbing in her room after you left. She was in such pain, physically and emotionally. She couldn't digest the aubergine pasta I made for lunch because of her distress. Thank god her mother came, or I wouldn't have known what to do. Whoever killed Pierre is still out there, and the trail is still hot. I wouldn't leave it up to chance. And Cyril and his team? That's chance."

"Now that you put it that way," Clémence said slowly, "I should do more. Since Cyril's grilling the coworkers, I can talk to Pierre's friends. Pierre's not very social, but if he's been friends with these two guys forever, he probably confides in them more. They're the only friends he has, apparently."

Berenice looked up. "Wait, but what if the killer is one of them?"

"I suppose it could be." Clémence thought about it a bit more. "Rose and I had left for Switzerland right after Rose got off work on Friday. She went home to get her stuff, so she saw him briefly to say good-bye. I waited in the taxi, so I didn't see him at all. Maybe I should ask her what happened the last time she saw him. Were his friends there? Pierre hangs out with his friends often, so since she was gone, it's likely that he would've spent his Friday night hanging with them. Maybe one or both of them ended up sleeping over."

"That would explain why Pierre wasn't surprised to have anyone in the house."

"Then either both guys were in on it, or only one."

"But if one did it, the other would know about it. It might've been an accident, you know?" Berenice said. "Maybe it happened when one of them was in a drunken stupor."

"It happened in the morning. They couldn't have still been drunk."

"True," said Berenice.

"So Friday evening, Pierre bought some food, which included a baguette from Damour. He went out with his friends, and maybe one of them crashed. The killer hit him on the head from behind with something hard, then fled. But why? I have to talk to these guys."

"*Tu as faim?*" Diane asked when Clémence returned. "Are you hungry?"

Two *pâtés aux pommes de terre* were fresh out of the oven, and two more were baking. "This looks and smells amazing."

The *pâté aux pommes de terre* was a potato pie. It was a specialty from Limousin, where Diane was from. With its delicious flaky pastry, crème fraîche, and slices of potatoes, nobody made a *pâté aux pommes de terre* quite like Diane did.

"Thanks." Diane beamed. "I'll serve it with a green salad for dinner. Will you be joining us?"

"Actually, I don't know. I just came back to ask Rose something, and I have to be on my way."

"What do you need? She still might not be feeling well. Is this something I can help you with?"

"Perhaps. I need Adam and Thierry's phone numbers. They're Pierre's best friends. I'm going to ask them some questions, and I also wanted to ask Rose more about them."

Diane hesitated. "You think this is a good time to ask Rose, sweetie? You might upset her even more."

Clémence sighed. "I know it's upsetting. She's your daughter. But time is of the essence. Pierre's killer is still out there. The sooner I find out, the sooner Rose will get closure."

"Don't you think the police should be the ones

doing the investigating? I heard you had some luck in the past, but criminal investigation is a dangerous field, chérie."

"I know it must look silly for a person like me to be trying to hunt down a murderer, but I can't stand back and do nothing. It just doesn't feel right."

"And you think Adam and Thierry might have information?"

"It doesn't hurt to try, right?"

Diane frowned, but she seemed to be considering her point of view. "Well, I suppose."

Suddenly, Rose came in. Her face was white, and there were dark rings under her eyes. Her blond hair was a mess from sleeping. However, there was a small smile on her face.

"Are you feeling better, Rose?" asked Diane.

"Yes. I smelled the dish all the way from my room. I've really missed your cooking, Mom."

She hugged Diane. Watching the loving mother and daughter, Clémence missed her own mother.

"You can learn how to make this," Diane said to Rose.

"I've tried, but it never comes out as good as yours, so what's the point?"

"It's a family recipe," said Diane. "You have to learn it so you can pass it down to your kids some-day." She turned to Clémence. "Does your mom cook,

Clémence? I know she's a famous baker, but does she make all the meals at home?"

"Sometimes," said Clémence. "And my father likes to cook, as well—at least, they did when I was growing up. When the patisseries took off, they had less time to do that, but we would just get our chefs to make our meals. They were my parents' recipes after all, and it was as good as homemade. We also ate at the *salon de thé* quite often, naturally. I couldn't expect my parents to cook all the time, since they work in the food industry for a living."

"So they do still get a sense of joy from cooking?" asked Diane.

"They do, and they are massive foodies. I work in the patisserie, and I'm never tired of baked goods, you know? They'll never get tired of cooking, at home or at work. It's just a matter of time."

Diane nodded. "I'm glad. My cooking was one of the reasons my ex-husband stayed with me for so long. He couldn't tell a spatula from a ladle in the kitchen. I keep telling Rose that the way to a man's heart is through his stomach, but you girls never seem to have time, these days."

"It's true," Clémence admitted. "I'm so busy these days that I just grab whatever I can, or I eat at the patisserie."

"Housewives are a dying breed," said Diane.

"Oh, Mom, you know we appreciate everything you do at home," said Rose. "Somebody has to do the things you do."

"Cooking is fine, but a housewife washes the floors, cleans the toilets—we're glorified housekeepers. I'm living off alimony, and it's not enough; but at my age, it's too late for me to get a job."

"I'm sure that's not true," Clémence said.

"A decent job, I mean. One where an education is required, which I don't have, but I'm so proud of you girls for being successful. At least I can be useful feeding you."

Diane's bitterness about the divorce came out from time to time. Clémence could understand. She had been with Mathieu for only three years before he dumped her for some nude model. After two years, Clémence was still bitter about it. Imagine if she had been married for two decades and had children with the man, and then found out that he had been cheating? She didn't know how Diane coped. She'd given the best years of her life to someone who chucked her for some cheap hussy.

This was why Clémence was so afraid of getting into another relationship. Deep down, love was what she wanted more than anything, but it was what she feared the most. That was why a simple lunch with Arthur could cause so much anxiety. Now that she thought about it a bit more, given Arthur's romantic history, who was to say that he wouldn't chuck her after one go, like he'd chucked all the other girls?

Well, she had to put a stop to this before anything was to start. She whipped out her phone and sent a quick text to Arthur.

Sorry, I changed my mind. I can't go to lunch with you. Let's just be friends.

Cold, but it was necessary to protect her heart. Maybe she'd meet the perfect guy who could prove himself to be trustworthy, one day. Maybe then she'd be more open to it. Besides, she had a full life, busy with her career, her friends—and, currently, the murder case.

"Rose, can you give me Adam and Thierry's numbers?" Clémence asked.

"To ask about—"

"Yes."

Reminded of Pierre, Rose gripped onto the kitchen counter and slowly nodded. "Of course."

"I need to know more about them," said Clémence. "Where they work, what they do, and all that."

"Well, Adam is all brawn. I actually think his brain is made out of muscle. He's a gym teacher in an elementary school in the sixth arrondissement, not far from where my apartment is. Thierry is an engineer working in healthcare technology, so he's smarter."

"They're all quite different, aren't they?" Clémence said.

"Sure are. They probably wouldn't be friends if they all met now, but they'd grown up together, and that kind of bond is stronger. Plus, they're all into soccer, rugby, and politics, so they have that in common."

"They know about the…death?"

"Yes," said Rose. "They both called me. I talked to each of them, but I kept it brief, since, you know, I don't want to talk about it detail."

"Of course." Clémence patted her on the shoulder. "I'm sorry you're going through this. I'll make sure that the murderer gets caught."

Clémence took down the name of Adam's school and Thierry's company name, as well as their contact information.

"Are you going to call them?" Diane asked.

"Actually, I think it's better if I meet them in person," said Clémence. "I'll start with the dumber one, Adam. If I pay him a surprise visit, I might catch him off guard."

CHAPTER NINE

*C*lémence entered the front doors of the École Elémentaire Paul Cézanne in the 6th arrondissement. Classes were already over, but Rose had told her that Adam worked after-school hours on Mondays and Wednesdays as part of the after-school program for the kids whose parents worked late and couldn't pick them up when classes ended. Many families in the wealthy arrondissement employed babysitters or nannies, since parents usually worked until seven p.m. or later, but some families preferred enrolling their kids in the program so they could get help with their homework or take part in Adam's sports program.

Clémence kept on the same outfit she'd worn to F.R. Fraser so she could look the part of a working mom and her presence wouldn't be questioned. She supposed she was old enough to have a child in elementary school, since she was twenty-eight.

Adam was in the playground area, blowing on his whistle as a dozen or so cute children skipped rope. She recognized Adam from the photos Rose had shown her on her smartphone. At six foot two, Adam had black hair and an overly toned upper body. He wore a ratty Rolling Stone T-shirt, blue gym shorts, and sneakers. She didn't mind watching the fit guy from the glass door as she waited for a chance to speak to him. When the children had some free time in the playground to choose and play their own activities, Adam went to the benches to sit down and drink some water.

Clémence took the opportunity to approach him. *"Vous êtes Adam?"*

"Oui." He gave her a quick once-over. The way his eyes widened conveyed that he liked what he saw.

"Je m'appelle Clémence. You don't know me, but I'm Rose's friend."

Adam stood up. *"Enchanté.* It's so unfortunate what happened to Pierre."

"Yes, and you can guess why I'm here."

"No, actually. Why are you here?"

Adam was pretty slow on the uptake. He was too hot to be smart. Paris, in general, was full of handsome men, but Adam possessed the movie-star kind of handsome, with his lean build and square jaw. Well, like the American movies, anyway. France hardly exported any real good-looking leading men. Her American girlfriends used to complain that it was a conspiracy, really—the good-looking guys in Paris were everywhere except on the big screen.

"I'm investigating Pierre's murder," Clémence said.

"Are you a cop?" Adam looked at her again more carefully. His eyes slid up her body slower this time.

"Will you cooperate if I said that I was?"

"Only if you handcuff me."

Clémence narrowed her eyes at him.

"I'm joking." He grinned.

"Do you know what happened to Pierre?" Clémence asked.

"I heard from his parents that he was killed in his apartment. Robbers are getting so crazy these days. I know two other people who'd been robbed this year, but this is the first time that I've heard of someone getting killed over it. I haven't even processed Pierre's death. It's so tragic."

"It wasn't a robber."

"It wasn't?"

"No. Nothing has been stolen."

"I just assumed," said Adam. "Then who would kill him?"

"That's why I'm here," said Clémence. "When was the last time you saw Pierre?"

"On Friday night. We went to the bars in the Latin Quarter."

"What time did you get home?"

"Not sure. I was pretty wasted."

"The others got wasted, as well?"

"Sure."

"Where did you go after?"

"Home. Thierry lives in the Seventeenth, but Pierre and I live close to each other. I think Pierre left first, though, so I didn't walk home with him."

"Why?"

"He got a call, and he left early."

Clémence frowned. "Who was the call from?"

"No clue. That's all I recall before we got those beers at this one bar and got really smashed."

"So Thierry stayed with you?"

"He did. We kept going until the bars closed late into the morning, then we sobered up a bit. We ate burgers and drank coffee. Then Thierry took a taxi home because he was falling asleep on me."

"Sounds like some boys' night out," Clémence said dryly. "Did you know that Pierre was killed on Saturday morning? Whoever he left you guys for probably had something to do with his death."

"You think so?" Adam asked. "Wow."

"That's right. Are you sure you don't have any clues as to who it was?"

"I have no idea. I thought it was Rose or something. Usually he goes home because of Rose."

"No, she was in Switzerland that weekend. You didn't know?"

"Oh, I guess I heard something about that, but I didn't make the connection."

"Unless..." Clémence said.

"What?"

"Do you know if Pierre was seeing someone on the side?"

Adam hesitated. "I—I don't know."

Clémence gave him a good hard look. "Are you sure? He's been with Rose for two years. You would know if he ever cheated on her, right?"

He was quiet for a moment. Clémence knew it: Adam knew something.

"Okay," he said, "but you won't tell Rose?"

"Look, Pierre is dead. Telling Rose would only hurt her. Help me out here. I'm trying to find Pierre's murderer."

Adam thought about it, then nodded. "Okay, well, sometimes we go clubbing. We'd talk to girls, buy them drinks or whatever. When Pierre's really drunk, he does let loose, and he has made out with some girls on the dance floor in the past."

"Girls, as in plural?"

Adam nodded. "He's young. It's harmless. As far as I know, Pierre has never gone home with them. Kissing was as far as it went."

"But you don't know that for sure."

"No, I guess not," he admitted.

"One of these girls could've gotten attached, maybe even killed him."

"Like a *Fatal Attraction* kind of thing?" Adam asked.

"Maybe. Do you know who any of these girls were?"

"No. They're just random club girls. We hit them and leave them."

"Classy," Clémence said. "What was Pierre's type?"

"Any girl, as long as she was attractive. He liked blondes."

It was too bad she couldn't go through Pierre's cell phone. The police had it.

"It's crazy." Adam shook his head. "I texted Pierre a couple of times this weekend, and he didn't respond. I thought it was weird, but figured he was busy. Now I know why."

"I'm sorry for your loss," Clémence said. "The inspector might want to ask you similar questions, if he ever comes around to it, just so you know."

"What inspector?"

"The one on the case."

"I thought you were on the case. So you're really not a cop?"

Clémence shook her head. He was as dumb as they came.

"Oh. You're too pretty to be a cop," Adam said. "But I'm disappointed. Hey, can I get your number? I can call you if I ever get more information."

Clémence wanted to turn him down, but she supposed that his having her number would help if Adam did have any new insights, however unlikely that was.

CHAPTER TEN

*C*lémence wanted—needed—the call log on Pierre's phone. Cyril hadn't contacted her or Rose with any follow-up questions, yet so he might've been busy with other leads. He was one of the last people on earth that she wanted to talk to, but this time, she needed his help. As much as it hurt her pride, she dialed his direct line.

"Oui?" came his gruff voice from the other end of the line.

"Bonsoir," Clémence tried to sound as polite as possible. "Clémence Damour here."

"Ah, *la heiress*. Are you calling with another Damour-related murder? I've got my hands full here."

"No, St. Clair," Clémence said through gritted teeth. "I called because I have some information. You'll need it. Where are you?"

"I don't see what I could possibly need. We're close to solving the case. We're just waiting for more evidence."

"Really?" she asked.

"Yes, really. Is that so hard to believe?"

"Actually, it is—"

St. Clair hung up. But Clémence knew where he was. She had heard the noise of the strike in the background. The taxi drivers were on strike in the 1st arrondissement, where he worked. She'd read about it on her phone while taking the Métro. Chances were he was in his office.

Since it was rush hour again, and taxis were probably scarce to none, she took the Métro to Cité and walked to 36 Quai des Orfèvres. On the third floor, she knocked on St. Clair's office door.

"There should really be better security in this building," Cyril muttered when he opened the door.

"Ironic," Clémence said, "since this is supposed to be the police headquarters."

"How did you get past the security?"

"Just slipped the guy twenty euros," said Clémence. "Just kidding. I just told the guy at the front desk that I had an appointment with you. If ever there was a benefit in being a young Caucasian woman, this is it."

He huffed. "You're supposed to wait in the

waiting room, and the receptionist is supposed to call me."

"Couldn't wait. They were too busy to notice anyway."

"The incompetency in this place." Cyril picked up the phone. "I'm calling security."

"Come on. We're peers now. I'm sure our case will go faster if we work together."

"Peers?" Cyril sneered. *"Our* case?"

Clémence suppressed a smile. It was too easy to toy with Cyril.

However, he also took every opportunity to peeve her. He got a knowing look on his face, and his scowl turned into a smile. "You'd usually go out of your way to avoid me, Damour. The fact that you're here tells me that you really want something from me."

"Wow," Clémence said. "Nothing gets past you does it, St. Clair?"

"It's *Monsieur* St. Clair."

"Stop calling me *'la heiress'* and maybe I'll consider it."

"Whatever you say, mademoiselle." He spat the word out of his mouth as if it were a derogatory remark. *"Dites-moi. Qu'est-ce que tu veux?"* What do you want?

"I didn't say you could *tutoyer* me," Clémence shot back, referring to the informal way people could address one another in the French language. "That's presumptuous of you."

"If you're comfortable enough to barge into my office, I think I have the right to call you 'tu'."

"But I'm young enough to be your daughter," she joked.

"Ha." Cyril was not amused. "You're trying to distract me. Out with it. It's late, and I want to get home."

"Long day? Who've you been chasing?"

"Nice try, Damour."

"Let me guess. Is it Mary, the assistant?"

Cyril's eyes widened. "How do you know that?"

"I saw you question her."

"You've been following me?"

"Please. I was there to question someone from the office, as well. In fact, I was there first. Now what do you have on Mary anyway? She seems like a nice gal."

Clémence was bluffing. She didn't know anything about Mary, but the more argumentative she was, the more likely Cyril would want to show off and prove her wrong.

He didn't fall for it this time, however. "Didn't you say you had something to tell me? Out with it!"

"Fine." Clémence told him about Adam and how someone had called Pierre on Friday, which caused him to leave his friends early. "Do you have Pierre's phone and computer? Did you find anything on it?"

"Yes." St. Clair sighed. "If you must know, we did follow up on one questionable call that showed up on his log. Other than that, this guy has no life outside of work and the same handful of people in his life."

"Well?" Clémence asked eagerly. "Who was this phone call from?"

"We tried to trace it, but it only went to a phone booth out of St. Lazare station."

"A phone booth? I didn't know there were any left in Paris."

"Exactly. It looks like whoever it was wanted to cover their tracks."

"Did you check the security cameras?"

"Yes. It was a woman wearing a big hat that obscured her face. She also wore sunglasses and gloves. Plus she was wearing a hideous dark overcoat that swallowed her shape. We couldn't tell who it was."

"But you could tell that this person was a woman," Clémence exclaimed. "This fits in with my theory that the killer was someone he was seeing on the side. The other woman."

"Hardly. There's no real evidence of that. This guy doesn't text, or even receives any texts from any women aside from Rose and his mother. We have reason to believe that it's Mary, the assistant. She doesn't have an alibi for Saturday, and on her work computer, we've found dozens of e-mails where she expresses hate for Pierre, and once, a threat to murder him."

"I did hear that he was a slave driver. Plenty of people are not crazy about him at F.R. Fraser, but would it really mean that this girl would kill him?"

"A regular employee wouldn't write e-mails saying she wants to choke their boss to death."

"Yeah, but a killer wouldn't, either. Sometimes employees need to vent."

"Damour, this is out of your league. It's her. Mary doesn't have an alibi for Friday night or Saturday morning. Said she was home alone, reading. She lives alone. There's no proof of her being anywhere, and she saw no one. Her only excuse was that she was so exhausted from the workweek that she simply went home on Friday night and slept for twelve hours, then proceeded to spend all of Saturday morning and afternoon at home. We're searching her house for further evidence and Pierre's DNA. We're questioning people in connection with her and Pierre. I'm sure we'll build a case against her to arrest her soon. The truth will come out."

"If you say so," said Clémence doubtfully.

"We've got this, Damour. Your services are not

needed. I always told you to leave the professionals to handle it. You got lucky with the two other cases. But that was all it was, luck. Your best use now is to be a pillow for your friend to cry on. Now get out of here, Damour. I don't want to see your face in here again."

Clémence stood up. She was glad that somebody was being held accountable. Mary did sound like the logical choice. Mary openly hated Pierre, made death threats, and was quite possibly the woman in the video footage who had called Pierre and lured him somewhere.

But what could she have said to make Pierre leave a bar on a Friday night? It didn't make complete sense yet.

CHAPTER ELEVEN

On Tuesday morning, Clémence joined Diane and Rose for breakfast. She would have suggested treating them to breakfast at Damour's *salon de thé*, but she was afraid that Rose would be triggered by Damour's association with Pierre's death. Clémence felt horrible that Rose might never want to eat at Damour again.

Rose looked better that morning. Her eyes were still a little swollen from crying, but she'd tried her best to put herself together. Her hair was styled into a sophisticated bun, she wore a bit of makeup, and she was dressed in a chic navy cashmere sweater and gray cigarette pants, and not the pajamas that she'd refused to change out of yesterday. At least she was making an effort to pull herself together.

"Why don't you tell Rose what you told me last

night?" Diane said to Clémence.

Rose jerked her head to Clémence. "What? Do the police have a lead?"

Clémence nodded. "Cyril is convinced it's Mary." She explained why.

"Well, what do you think?" Rose looked at Clémence closely.

Although something didn't feel right with Cyril's conclusion, it wasn't as if Clémence had ideas of her own. It could've been her ego talking; she didn't want Cyril to be right on some level because they'd been sparring for so long. She also had not met Mary, so who was she to say? Could Cyril actually be right for once?

"I don't know," Clémence said. "It could be her. What do you think?"

"I'm not sure, either," said Rose. "I met Mary very briefly once when I visited Pierre at the office. She was reasonably helpful to me. Pierre detested her, though, but would she detest him back to the point where she would murder him?"

Clémence did not want to tell her what Adam had told her. It was a possibility that Mary could've had an affair with Pierre, and perhaps if he had broken it off, her heart had been broken.

"Clémence told me that this girl has no alibi for Friday night or Saturday," said Diane. "Sounds pretty suspicious to me. I'm sure that once they prove it's her, you'll begin to put this whole episode behind you, Rose."

"I don't know if that's possible," Rose said. "Pierre died in Daddy's apartment. I saw his body. I can't go back there again."

"I'm sure we can convince your father to sell the apartment. I've always hated that apartment. He used to take that bimbo there, the woman he left me for." Diane clutched her napkin hard. She turned to Clémence. "Did you know that he got the apartment when we were married, and I didn't know about it? They could've had their secret meetings in hotels, but no, he needed an apartment. Who knows how long it would've gone on if I hadn't caught them in the act?"

Rose put a hand on Diane's. "I know, Mom. I'm sorry."

Clémence didn't know how to respond. It was awkward whenever Diane's bitterness about her divorce flared up. She used to be such a happy, vibrant woman. Clémence hoped that she could get over it, but it seemed doubtful that she would, since it had been years now. Maybe Clémence and Rose could do something nice for her, like take her back to the hotel spa in Zurich.

The doorbell rang.

"I'll get it, girls," Diane said. "Finish up your

breakfast."

Clémence didn't have much of an appetite. She hoped that she was wrong about Pierre cheating on Rose. She'd already witnessed how infidelity had wrecked her mother. Rose would be incredibly hurt to find out that the only man she'd ever loved had been lying and cheating on her.

"Clémence." Diane stuck her head back into the kitchen with a conspiratorial grin on her face. "There's a gentleman friend here for you."

Rose raised an eyebrow at Clémence.

"I'll be right back," said Clémence.

"You didn't tell me that this Arthur was so cute," Diane whispered to her in the hall. "I invited him in. He's in the salon."

Clémence turned red. She really hoped that he didn't hear what Diane just said. The walls in the apartment were so thin. Through the glass door to the salon, she saw his profile. Clean shaven and wearing an azure blue shirt and black dress pants, he looked as gorgeous as ever. When she came in, he stood up.

"I'll leave you two alone," said Diane. Her gaze lingered on Arthur before she retreated back into the kitchen.

Clémence closed the salon door, not that it would help much. Diane and Rose could probably hear them from the kitchen if they left the door open, which she was sure Diane would do.

"What are you doing here?" she asked Arthur.

"Nice to see you, too," he said. "I got your text, and I texted you back. I even called you, but you didn't pick up."

"Oh. I've been busy."

"What happened yesterday to change your mind?" He stepped closer, overwhelming her with his warmth. Instinctively, she stepped back.

"I just realized that dating a neighbor would be a bad idea."

"Come on, Clémence. We both like each other. I definitely know that you're into me."

"How so?" She crossed her arms.

He chuckled. "By the way you look at me. I'm not impervious to the effect I have on women."

"Oh please, Guillaume Canet," she teased, referring to the only French movie star she found remotely attractive. He smiled in his cocky way that she didn't know whether she found adorable or extremely irritating. This was the kind of guy she needed to guard herself against. She wasn't going to be played like Diane or Rose. "You're not my type."

Arthur gave her a doubtful look. "What's your type? Tall, handsome, educated, well-dressed, confident, rich?"

"Somebody who doesn't irritate me," she shot back.

"I was planning on taking you to SushiSalsa," he said. "The new restaurant near Victor Hugo that everyone's talking about. You heard about that place, right?"

"I can't," Clémence said, even though she was tempted. She'd been wanting to try SushiSalsa.

"Why? Are you still investigating leads on this case? How's it going, by the way?"

"Fine. The police are handling it."

"The police?" Arthur burst into a laugh. "It's not like you to let the police do their job. Something's up."

"No, everything's fine," said Clémence. "It's under control."

Arthur examined her for a second longer. "Okay, forget about lunch. But look, it's a beautiful day. Why don't we go take a walk? You look tense. Maybe some fresh air will do you good."

"Tense?" She scowled at him.

"Still beautiful," he said quickly. "You look beautiful."

Clémence considered the offer. She did want to take a walk. What was the harm in that?

"Fine," she said. "Let's go. Just a short walk."

CHAPTER TWELVE

*C*lémence and Arthur walked down Avenue Kléber towards the Arc de Triomphe, the grand monument at Place Charles de Gaulle.

"Have you ever been up there?" Arthur asked.

"The Arc de Triomphe? Yes, a couple of times. Have you?"

"I've never been up."

Clémence gave him a surprised look. "Why not?"

"It's a touristy thing to do."

"Well, have you been up the Eiffel Tower?" she asked.

"Of course not. Have you seen the line-ups?"

"It's why I haven't been up, either," said Clémence. "I'm content just to look at the tower."

"Same here."

The truth was, Clémence had plenty of opportunities to go up the Eiffel Tower. Whenever she had friends or her American cousins in Paris to visit her, she'd been invited to go up the tower with them, but she never did. It wasn't that she didn't want to or minded the crazy lines. She had just always wanted to save the occasion for when she found the love of her life.

Deep down, she was a romantic. She held on to the idea of a special "one", someone who deserved to go up the tower with her. She'd never told anyone this desire.

She had almost made it up with her ex, Mathieu, but something had always gotten in the way: a sudden rainstorm, Mathieu complaining about the tourists and the long lines, a last-minute invitation to go somewhere else. Their relationship just hadn't been meant to be; she could see that now.

"It's funny." She smiled at Arthur. "You live so close to the Eiffel Tower and the Arc de Triomphe, yet you have never been up either."

"Anything to avoid the tourists," said Arthur.

"You're a true Parisian," Clémence teased.

"Well, I think there are better views of Paris, like on top of the George Pompidou, or the roof of Galerie Lafayette."

"Or from the Sacré-Cœur," said Clémence.

"I rarely go to that section of Montmartre."

Arthur crinkled his nose. "But you're right. It is funny that I've never been up the Arc. What do you say we go up now?"

"Why now?"

He shrugged. "Since you're with me, it might be nice."

"I thought you hated tourist stuff."

"I can't let some dumb people in horrid sandals and oversized cameras stop me from enjoying my own city. Come on."

"Okay, but I'll warn you, there are a lot of stairs to climb."

"No need to worry." Arthur grinned. "I'm incredibly fit."

The Arc de Triomphe stood in the middle of the Place Charles de Gaulle, a large road junction where twelve avenues intersected. The avenues met at the Arc, forming a star shape, and it was essentially a huge roundabout that they had no way of crossing. Instead, there was an underground passageway to enter the Arc.

The Arc was built to honor those who fought during the French Revolution, and it stood 164 feet tall. The tourists on the streets were snapping away, in awe of its size. Clémence had been up once during a school trip when she was eleven, and another time when her American cousins came to visit when she was sixteen. Both times, she'd been thoroughly impressed by the view from the top. The second time she'd visited, the sun had been setting, and the skyline had been washed in pinks and purples; the city really lived up to its own image of beauty.

As she walked with Arthur, she appreciated the perfect weather. No sign of rain clouds, which were constantly threatening the state of the weather and the moods of the city's inhabitants. There was a line, but it was a Tuesday morning, so it wasn't as long as it was at peak times. After waiting for ten minutes, during which she and Arthur soaked in their surroundings and Arthur even managed to crack a few funny jokes and made her laugh, they got to the ticket booth. Arthur insisted on paying for them.

"You really don't have to," Clémence said. After all, it wasn't a date. Just a friendly stroll.

"I know I don't have to. I want to. Besides, you'll owe me."

"Owe you?" She lightly smacked him on the chest.

"Yes, when we get to the top, you'll have to kiss me."

Clémence laughed. She wondered what had gotten into Arthur lately. He'd loosened up and gotten more comfortable around her. He could really turn on the charm when he wanted to; she could see why he was such a ladies' man.

"We'll see if you can get to the top without panting," said Clémence.

Sure enough, the long, dark and dank staircase took a toll on him—on the both of them—after a few minutes of climbing. They stopped near the top, where they watched a video about the Arc's history and poked around the souvenir shop. Arthur bought a 3-D Arc de Triomphe puzzle for his younger brothers. If he had done that even partly to make Clémence's heart melt, he had succeeded.

"There's something different about you, these days," she said. "You're not insulting me and making snotty comments—not as much as you used to, anyway. You're actually nice. What's gotten into you?"

Instead of answering, he simply gazed deep into her eyes. His irises were so brown and warm. His body was mere inches from her, and she could smell his aftershave. His gaze moved down to her lips, and he leaned in, closer and closer.

Then suddenly, he backed off. "Come on."

He squeezed her hand and pulled her to the staircase, where they continued up to the very top.

Crowds of tourists admired the view of the streets below, as well as the sky and city that were open all around them.

Arthur and Clémence didn't exude the same awe as the visitors, since they did have stunning views of the city already from their balconies. However, to be in the center of the "star" of the twelve streets was fun. She especially loved looking out to Rue Champs-Elysées, the famous boulevard with its perfectly manicured trees.

Arthur pointed out La Defense in the northwest, poking fun at how industrial and futuristic it looked compared to central Paris. Under the sunny blue sky, the rooftops of the Haussuman buildings were more blue than gray, and the trees looked more lush and green. The city was really a photographer's dream.

"Do you think Paris is more beautiful when it's sunny or in the rain?" Arthur asked.

Clémence took a moment to ponder the question. "I don't know." She sighed. "I just love Paris. I'll take the city anytime, as it is."

"It's funny. You're French, but you're still in love with Paris."

"But I love Paris not the way a vacationer would. I love Paris unconditionally. I accept the good and the bad. Besides, I grew up in the suburbs, so I don't take everything for granted like you do. What do you think? Sun or rain?"

"The weather changes its mood," said Arthur. "When it's sunny, like today, it's full of hope and happiness. People are out. They're more relaxed. When it rains, it's romantic as well, but in a somber, melancholy way. The way you feel watching a black-and-white movie. The only time when I don't think Paris is pretty is when the sky is entirely overtaken by gray clouds. Then everything is dreary. Personally, I prefer Paris in the sun. Because, right now, your face is all lit up, and you seem to be glowing."

He leaned in and kissed her. His lips were soft and grazed over hers ever so slightly, until he pulled her in and pressed against her. She felt the heat start from the lips, spreading down to her chest until her entire body was tingling.

When they pulled away, Clémence couldn't look at him. It was everything a first kiss should be, and she needed to recover so Arthur wouldn't see how much he'd affected her. She looked around at the other tourists. At least two other couples were making out, as well.

Clémence let out an embarrassed laugh. Arthur followed her gaze to one of the couples, kissing furiously.

"They look like they're trying to bite each other's heads off," he mused. "Don't you wish that we didn't have to share this city with all these people?"

Clémence imagined a city devoid of people. "No. It's not so bad. I'd rather be bombarded by cheesy tourists under the spell of the city, rather than the jaded French. Their optimism balances out our extreme cynicism. Although we do fall under the spell of the city when we're not careful. Right now, I feel like a tourist, like everyone else here. I'm surprised you're so taken with this place, too."

"I'm taken with you," he said. "You asked what's gotten into me earlier. Well, it's you. At first, I don't know, I didn't think much of it—us, I mean. Sure, you were cute, but plenty of girls are cute."

"Thanks a lot," she said.

"But the more I got to know you, the more I started to like you. Then I got to the point when I just couldn't stop thinking about you. There's just something about you that makes me want to, I don't know, be more kind around you."

Clémence chuckled. "That's actually kind of sweet. You know, you can be nice when you want to be."

"And like I said, I stopped messing around with those other girls. It just started feeling so empty after a while, being with a girl I can't even have a conversation with."

"You think we have good conversations?"

"You challenge me. Sure, you seem to know nothing about macroeconomics, but at this point, it's not like it's something I want to talk about since I'm working on it day and night. You're creative and clever, and that intrigues me. Besides, I like tagging along with your misadventures, even though you drive me crazy sometimes."

Clémence felt her cheeks getting warm. "Thanks."

"You look pretty when you blush."

She looked down.

"There's also something pure about you. You're not like the other French girls. You're a bit prudish, which is surprising in this day and age."

"I get it from my father," she said.

Arthur laughed. Clémence hadn't been joking, however. Her dad had very conservative values, and he had probably passed them down to Clémence. She believed in monogamy, in not smoking, in not drinking too much, in being fair and kind to others.

"Clémence, I really want to give this try."

"You mean…"

"I know we live in the same building, but it can work. I won't be dropping in all the time, if that's what you're worried about. We both have lives. I want to see you more. Go out for dinner and see what happens."

"I thought it was lunch."

"That was before we kissed. We're on a dinner basis now, don't you think?"

Think? Clémence's logical side told her to calm down, to consider the consequences. But the other side, her instinctual side, was screaming oui. Arthur didn't give her a chance to reply, because he said, "Okay, fine, I am getting hungry. If you insist, let's go to lunch."

Clémence smiled. "You're a real con artist, you know that?"

CHAPTER THIRTEEN

SushiSalsa was a new restaurant on Avenue Victor Hugo. While there were new sushi places popping up in Paris every day, SushiSalsa was upscale, offering intricately made sushi platters. When the waiter brought their orders, which came in wooden boats, Clémence beamed.

"It certainly smells good," Clémence said. "Hey, I wonder if a line of sushi-flavored macarons would take off at Damour."

"Fish-flavored macarons?"

Clémence made a face. "Well, it doesn't sound good, but we've had success with savory macarons in the past. I know other patisseries have wasabi-flavored ones."

"I think you're just inspired by the visually pleasing display of our sushi."

"Trust me," said Clémence. "We could pull it off. Savory macarons make great starters."

"I don't doubt you for a moment." Arthur grinned.

She took a bite of her avocado and fried shrimp sushi, and she suppressed a moan of pleasure. The pieces were drizzled with a creamy, spicy sauce with pepper flakes, which gave the right amount of kick.

Arthur took a bite, coughed, and chugged down his glass of water.

"Too spicy for you?" Clémence asked.

Many French people couldn't handle food that was very spicy. Clémence had built up her tolerance when she traveled through Asia last year. Now she loved spicy food. Arthur obviously did not. He finished the entire bottle of sparkling water that they had been sharing and asked for another.

"I didn't think it would be that spicy." His face flushed red, and there were beads of sweat on his forehead and above his upper lip.

Clémence tried not to laugh; she thought Arthur was even more adorable when he couldn't keep up his cool act.

"Why are you smiling?" he asked. "Are you laughing at me?"

"No. I was just thinking that you're kind of cute."

"When I'm acting foolish?"

"Yes."

"Maybe I should act foolish more often."

"I don't think you need to try."

He laughed. He picked out the spicy sushi pieces from his boat dish and gave them to her. "You'll obviously enjoy them more than I will. You wouldn't want me to pass out on our first lunch date, wouldn't you?"

"Fine, I'll take them, if only to save your life."

The waiter came with a new bottle of water, and Arthur poured himself another glass to chug down.

"Speaking of lives," Arthur said slowly, "how is your friend Rose handling all this?"

"Just hanging in there. I'm hoping that once they arrest the killer, she'll start to get over her grief. It's going to take some time, but..."

Clémence frowned and looked into space.

"What are you thinking, Damour?" Arthur said. "I know that look."

"It's just that something feels wrong about this. The police are trying to build a case against Mary. I do hope that it is her, but something about it just doesn't feel right to me."

"Why?"

"I don't know. I haven't talked to the girl, so I'm not confident about my theory."

"Why haven't you talked to her? You're usually on any potential suspects like white on rice."

Clémence thought about it. He was right. Why was she avoiding Mary?

"I guess I want the killer to be her," she finally said.

"But you really don't think it's her."

"No. Cyril is certain, but he's been wrong before. Her motive is not very strong. It's not unusual for people to hate their bosses and to complain about them to their coworkers and friends. It would take a certain kind of person to break into the boss's home and kill them when they're having breakfast. Cyril thinks the murder was calculated, but I don't think it is. I think it's a crime of passion. Unless they can find out that Mary had an affair or something with Pierre, I doubt that it's her."

"It did happen in the morning," Arthur said, "when the guy was in his pajamas. It does sound more likely that the killer would've been someone he'd just slept with and trusted to be in his apartment."

Clémence nodded. "When St. Clair sets his sights on someone, he's too stubborn to give it up. He hates to be wrong. The only real evidence we have is the security footage. The woman really took precautions to go undetected. I'm sure they've searched the apartment for fingerprints and DNA, and they're now trying to match it up with Mary's, but if they don't find a match—and the more I think on it, the less I think they will—they're going to be back at square one."

"You really have no other suspects?" Pierre asked.

"No. Pierre had girls on the side—I'm sure he had more than one. He's a very discreet guy."

"Nobody is that discreet. I'm sure there's a way of finding out who these girls are."

"You're right. I haven't tried everything. I guess I just didn't want to be right. Rose is my best friend. If I find the truth, I'd break her heart. To find out that your dead boyfriend was cheating on you before he died?"

Clémence shook her head. She'd eaten less than half her meal, but she had already lost her appetite.

"She deserves to know the truth," Arthur argued. "Don't think of it as breaking her heart. Think of it as setting her free. Then she wouldn't put him on a pedestal. People tend to make saints out of the dead."

"True. They had been fighting, but all she talks about now are his good qualities. All she has are good memories. I guess I wanted her to keep that illusion."

"I don't know if that's healthy."

"It probably isn't." Clémence sighed. "I do want to look more into his computer, but the police has it."

"What's on his computer?"

"I wanted to check his e-mails. Maybe there's a

clue that the police overlooked. It could be easier to trace an e-mail, if I find something incriminating. Maybe they've been so focused on Mary's communication with him that they overlooked some other e-mails."

"Can you ask Rose if she has his password information?"

"You think she'll have it?" Clémence asked.

"You'll be surprised. A few years ago, my ex demanded that I give her all the passwords to my e-mails, Facebook, and other accounts. She was really possessive and had trust issues. I ended up giving her one password to an e-mail I used mainly to receive junk mail."

"Wow. I didn't know you were in a relationship. Why did you do it?"

Arthur sighed. "I was in love with her. And I wanted her to trust me, but she turned out to be crazy. Nothing satisfied her, and I had no choice but to break up with her."

"That really did a number on you, huh?"

"She put me off relationships, definitely. She was needy, clingy, and jealous. She used to have a life before me, but she dropped her friends and her passions to focus on me and our relationship. That could get old, fast."

"Right."

Had Clémence made the same mistake with Mathieu? Perhaps. She always believed that he was the talented one, the one destined for greatness in the art world. Maybe subconsciously, she had prepared herself to be the muse, the wife to support the genius. As a result, he got bored and took her for granted. He cheated on her.

"But you're different," said Arthur. "You're opinionated, you have your own interests, and you don't seem to be the clingy, jealous type."

"I'm not interested in living someone else's life," she said. And she meant it. A relationship didn't mean one person making all the sacrifices. It was the wrong way to think. She'd learned her lesson. At least from the horrible experience with Mathieu, she knew to never let a man take her for granted.

Arthur looked at her with admiration. "It's why I like you, Damour."

CHAPTER FOURTEEN

"*R*ose?" Clémence called out when she came home. "Are you here?"

"*Oui.*" Footsteps came from the hallway to the bedrooms, and Rose's elfin face emerged near the entrance. She was wearing a snuggly blue bathrobe and fluffy pink slippers.

"There you are," said Clémence.

"I was in the bath. You're right. A bath with lavender Epsom salts feels really amazing. My muscles are so relaxed. It's the next best thing to being at the spa."

"Feels like a lifetime ago now, doesn't it?"

Rose nodded. There was still a trace of sadness on her face.

Clémence wished her friend could be happy again. "Where's your mom?"

"Out buying groceries. I hope you don't mind that she's here."

"Of course I don't mind. You can both stay for as long as you like. Actually, there's something I wanted to talk to you about."

"What is it?" Rose frowned.

They went into the kitchen and sat down at the table.

"I was wondering if you had Pierre's e-mail password?"

"I don't," she said. "He was very private about those things. Why?"

"Well, I just want to make sure that the police are on the right track."

"You're not sure his assistant did it, are you?"

"Not completely."

"I didn't think you did. I was thinking about it in the bath. Something doesn't feel right about it. Pierre had never gotten along with Mary professionally, but that's common in a high-pressure workplace. Would she really come to his house and kill him just because she was working overtime? I mean, she could quit, right?"

"Right," said Clémence. "I checked out her LinkedIn profile, and it sounds like she's quite educated. She could easily quit or transfer if she really hated her position. She has options."

"But who else could it be?"

"That's why I wanted to check Pierre's e-mails. What if there's something that the police overlooked? I know they confiscated his laptop and phone, but I was hoping there was another way to access his account."

"Unfortunately, I don't have his passwords. I think he has an e-mail for work and a private e-mail. The one for work could be accessed on his laptop, or his boss would probably have access to it, as well."

"I suppose I can visit his workplace again and ask, although..."

"Wait! Pierre does have an iPad. He keeps it in a blue sleeve and I'm pretty sure it's still shoved between books on our bookshelf. It might still be at the apartment."

"Do you need a password to access the iPad?"

"Yes, but I know this password. It's the year of his birth, nineteen eighty-six. He doesn't know that I know, but I happened to be over his shoulder when he was punching it in and I saw it by accident. Maybe his e-mail is accessible without a password on the iPad."

"I'll have to go get it right away, then. Do you still have the key to the apartment?"

"Yes." Rose went to the coat closet near the front

door and found her key ring. "The big key is for the entrance, and this one is for the apartment."

"I'll go there now."

"Are you sure it's safe?"

"I doubt the police are still there."

"I'd offer to go with you, but..."

"I understand," Clémence said. "It's painful for you. Don't worry. I won't be long."

As Clémence approached Rose's former apartment, she wondered if she should've called a guy friend to come with her for protection just in case. She sure had needed it on her last two cases.

She brushed off her worries; she would be fine. What was there to worry about? It wasn't as if the killer was still lurking in the apartment. She would just get the iPad and get out.

As she went up the staircase, she wondered if St. Clair had already interrogated all the neighbors. Had they heard anything that night? Like many of the old buildings in Paris, the walls were thin. At Clémence's apartment, sometimes when she was sitting quietly in the kitchen alone, she could hear the couple below arguing. Perhaps a neighbor had done the same to

Pierre, mistaking the woman he was having an affair with for Rose.

She put the keys in the hole and turned. Inside the apartment, the windows were still closed, leaving a musty smell. Pierre was gone, but his breakfast was still there. They'd just left it there. Were they expecting Rose to clean this up? The bread was probably as hard as a rock now.

The apartment was deathly quiet. It felt wrong to be there—and spooky, as somebody she knew had died there. She better make it quick.

In Rose and Pierre's bedroom, she found the iPad on the shelf. She took it out of its blue sleeve. It still had power, and it turned on when she pressed the Home button. She punched in the code, and it unlocked. Her original plan had been to get the iPad and get out, but she was too eager to look through its contents right away. The account the iPad was linked to was Pierre's personal e-mail.

She sat down on the chair at his desk and began to read through them. In his inbox were exchanges with friends, Rose, and his family, and various forwards and e-mail subscriptions. In the "Sent" box, Clémence learned he wasn't much of an e-mailer. He probably did so much e-mailing at work that he didn't do much of it in his spare time. Perhaps it was why the woman called him instead.

She looked for e-mails to other women. He'd often responded to his mother, Rose, and a couple of female names Clémence didn't recognize. After going through them, she pieced together that one of them was his cousin and another was an aunt. Then finally she found an e-mail from someone named "Samantha Xes".

"Xes" wasn't a typical French surname, as far as Clémence knew. It was not a name she'd heard of in general.

It suddenly came to her that "Xes" was "sex" spelled backwards. That was the first clue.

The e-mail was short: *Pierre, went to the Ritz for coffee, and it reminded me... SX.*

Reminded her of what? The Ritz was a hotel. Perhaps they had a rendezvous there?

She searched his e-mails for more Samantha Xes e-mails. There were only two more, the first being from a year ago. It said, *Tea and croissants this Friday? Same place. SX.*

The second was from four months ago. *Really can't get enough of those pastries. SX.*

Three e-mails, in the span of a year. Perhaps they had met more than three times. She noticed that Pierre never even replied to these e-mails. He just received them. Maybe he replied in other ways. They were both private and sneaky.

Who was Samantha Xes? She searched the name on Google, but the results came back with nothing. It must've been a code name. This woman really went out of her way to protect her identity.

Clémence needed to convince Cyril St. Clair to help her track this woman down; she didn't have the technical skills to do so. She breathed a sigh of relief that she had a new lead: she was one step closer to getting justice for Rose.

Before she left, she took another look around the apartment. She put on leather gloves as she searched just in case. The police probably did all the searching and took all the samples they needed, but if they could miss these e-mails, they might've missed other things. Perhaps Pierre had left some clues by mistake. Perhaps the woman had, since she'd been in the apartment.

Clémence looked in the closet, under the bed, behind the couch. All she could find was Rose's blond hair. Unless the other woman had blond hair as well —Adam did mention that Pierre had a thing for blondes.

In the kitchen, she checked all the cupboards. It would've been easier if Rose was here to help her, so she could point out anything that was unusual or out of place.

She checked the fridge. There were a few rotting

vegetables, condiments, and leftovers in a reheatable glass container. Clémence opened the container. Inside was a piece of *pâté aux pommes de terre*, just like the one Diane made yesterday. It still looked edible, and it must've been made recently. Did Rose make it before she left for Zurich? She couldn't have, because Rose proclaimed she didn't know how to make the dish well. Perhaps she was just being modest, or she had brought some home earlier in the week when she visited her mother.

Clémence would have to ask Rose about this. She decided that since she was here, she might as well start interrogating the neighbors. She chose the apartment that was closest to the Rose's bedroom. There was a chance that they might've heard what happened that night.

She knocked on the door. A housekeeper answered. She was a stout, middle-aged lady with her graying hair in a messy bun, and she spoke French with a Polish accent.

"The owners are not here," she told her.

"When will they be back?"

"Maybe half an hour."

"Oh. Do you mind if I wait here?"

"Okay. I can give them a call to let them know you are here. What is your name?"

"Clémence. They don't know me, but I'm actually

a friend of their neighbor, Rose. I have some very important questions to ask them."

The housekeeper tried one number and left a voicemail message. She tried another number, but no one picked up, either.

Clémence picked up one of the magazines on the coffee table and waited the half hour. Then it turned into an hour. She figured that she should just leave her card. Who knew when they were going to be back? She could be spending her valuable time interviewing others, especially Mary.

She had some Damour business cards in her bag, but she realized that she'd left the bag in Rose's apartment. Following the excitement of her new discovery on Pierre's iPad, she was careless enough to forget her bag. She told the housekeeper that she would be right back.

When she took out the key, which she had kept in her jean pocket, she heard shuffling noises.

Somebody was in Rose's apartment.

Whoever it was stopped moving.

"St. Clair?" she called from the door. "Is that you?"

Nobody answered.

The floor squeaked in the kitchen. A face emerged.

"You," Clémence exclaimed, half surprised and half not.

CHAPTER FIFTEEN

*D*iane stood before her wearing a black, cape-like coat and black leather gloves. Her blond hair was tucked under a floppy black hat. It was similar outfit to the one worn by the woman in the security footage at St. Lazare, from how St. Clair had described it.

"Are you surprised?" Diane asked.

Clémence left the front door open, wishing that she had brought a bodyguard with her, after all. She was standing in an empty apartment with a killer, someone she'd known since she was thirteen. The Polish housekeeper next door had begun to vacuum. Although the door was open, she wondered if the other neighbors were home, and whether they'd be able to hear their conversation. She decided to speak as loud as possible.

"I am surprised." Clémence was also surprised by the calmness of her voice. "Although, a part of me isn't. That *pâté aux pommes de terre* was from you, wasn't it? You made it for Pierre."

"Clever girl." Diane crossed her arms. Her face twisted into a snarl. "I also bought the baguette. I'm a big fan of your baguettes."

Clémence shook her head sadly. "You're Rose's mother. I wanted to give you the benefit of the doubt."

Diane sneered. "Oh, Clémence. You've always been a Goody-Two-Shoes, a real pushover. Haven't you learned? My daughter certainly hasn't. Trust no one."

"Why would you do this?" Clémence exclaimed.

"Why? Why do we do anything? Why do we live? Why do we die? Why do we laugh or cry? There's no reason to do anything anymore, so I took what was mine. I took whatever joy I could find that was left in this world."

"By stealing your daughter's boyfriend?"

"I wasn't stealing him. What doesn't belong to you can't be stolen, right? That's what my ex-husband always said."

"You're sick. You need help."

"Pierre knew what he was doing. A year ago, I happened to run into him at Galerie Lafayette, in the lingerie department. He was shopping for Rose, but once we locked eyes, that was it. We got a hotel room that same afternoon, and we snuck away whenever Rose wasn't around. He liked older woman. He couldn't get enough of me."

"But how could you do that to Rose?"

"Rose has a lifetime to find boyfriends. She's young. What about me? I'm in my fifties. Sex with someone like Pierre isn't going to come by for long. I had to take what was mine."

"But Rose wanted to marry him!"

"Pierre was scum, anyway. He was going to cheat on her. And he treated me like crap after he was done with me. Rose should be so lucky to get rid of him. I know I am. You know what he said after he had his way with me on Friday? He said he was done with me. Of course I didn't believe him."

"You didn't want to believe him, you mean."

"He said that it was over, that he never wanted to see me again. After a night of passion that we had? In the morning, he had the nerve to toss me out like garbage. When I wouldn't listen, he said that he doesn't want me because I was an old hag. That I was all used up and that he never wanted to see me again. Well. I clunked him over the head with my purse. It was an accident. I didn't realize there were so many things in my bag, like a hardback book and all my beauty products. I just wanted to hurt him, but when he wasn't getting up, it felt good. I was actually glad. I laughed. After all he'd said and done, I don't feel remorse at all. He deserved it entirely."

"Why did you come here?" Clémence asked, even though she had an idea. "Why did you come to the scene of the crime? Did you want to get caught?"

"Rose told me you came here to get the iPad. I figured you'd be gone by now, so I came here to see if the piece of pâté aux pommes de terre was still there. I had meant for Pierre to eat it, but that was before I killed him. When Rose said you were coming, I remembered that it was probably still in the fridge, the only thing connecting me to the murder. It sounded like no one was in the apartment when I came here, so I let myself in."

"So you have a spare key to the apartment."

"It was how I caught my husband. When I found out that he was spending money on another apartment, I found the extra key in his briefcase, made the copy, and one day, I was here, catching him in the act with some dirty little slut."

"Diane. You really need help, and you're not going to get away with this."

She laughed, cackled really. "I already have."

"The police are on their way," Clémence bluffed.

"I don't think so, little girl. Not if I kill you first."

Diane pulled a knife from one of the massive pockets of her coat, then the knife was coming down on Clémence's chest.

CHAPTER SIXTEEN

*C*lémence jumped out of the way. The knife stabbed the counter instead. Diane cried out from the pain of hitting something solid and attempted to stab her again, but Clémence punched her right on the face.

"Ouch!" Clémence muttered. "That really hurt my knuckles."

Diane dropped her knife. Blood gushed from her nose. "You broke my nose, you bitch!"

Clémence kicked the knife away, then retrieved it. Clémence backed out into the hallway as Diane covered her nose, wailing. The Polish housekeeper came out, asking what all the commotion was about. Clémence asked her to call the police.

Diane wouldn't be going anywhere, especially with a broken nose—Clémence would make sure of that. She needed medical treatment, then some jail time.

"Are you crazy, Clémence? You almost got yourself killed again?"

Arthur looked mad and relieved at the same time. The police had arrested Diane, who at first insisted on her innocence, but after Clémence listed all the evidence: the *pâté aux pommes de terre* in the fridge, the e-mails, the confession she'd heard, the stabbing attempt, and the fact that she'd shown up at the apartment, Diane relented and confessed all over again to Cyril and his team. Cyril was proud to arrest the killer, but annoyed that he hadn't been the one to catch her—again.

After they took Diane away, Clémence went outside for some air. She met Arthur on the street, as she'd texted him and he'd come as soon as he could.

"It's not like I throw myself into these kinds of situations," she said.

"What did I tell you before? If you ever need someone to help you, you can call me."

"Sorry. I didn't know it was going to be dangerous. It was supposed to be an in-and-out operation. Plus, we just saw each other, and I didn't want to be needy."

"You have a lot of pride, you know that, Damour?" Arthur gave her a reassuring kiss. "Are you sure you're not bleeding or bruised anywhere?"

"No, I'm fine. My hand hurts from punching her nose, but I'm really okay."

He broke out into a smile. "I can't believe you broke her nose."

"She deserves it." Clémence sighed. "I don't know how I'm going to tell Rose. Her mother not only had sex with her boyfriend for a year, but she killed him. Now she's going to jail. How is Rose supposed to take this?"

"I don't know." Arthur held her in a tight embrace.

"And how could Diane do this? I've known her since I was thirteen! I can't believe people can turn into psychopaths."

"Well, I'm sure it was gradual. Heartbreak really messes some people up."

"Some people get over it," Clémence said. "They move on. I guess this is what happens when people let anger and bitterness ravage their souls."

Clémence realized that she had been nervous. Sure, she'd acted calm when she defended herself, but now that she was in Arthur's arms, she realized how shaken she really was.

She pulled back, looking deep into Arthur's eyes. "Will you come with me to break the news to Rose? I don't think I can do it alone."

"Sure," he said, and he kissed her eyelid.

CHAPTER SEVENTEEN

one week later

*C*lémence went to the Damour kitchen to check up on the bakers. She was itching to work on the new savory line of sushi macarons, but Sebastien and Berenice were busy making éclairs. She felt as if she hadn't been at work in forever, after all that had happened.

Rose had broken down and cried for two days after she learned about her mother. It was painful, but at least it gave her closure on one part of her life with Pierre. Now she would face the pain of having her mother going on trial for murder, and then having a mother in prison. Clémence offered her apartment for Rose to stay in for as long as she wanted, but Rose needed to be with family, so Clémence helped Rose pack to live in Germany with her father for a while.

After Rose left, Clémence was able to see Arthur more often. They would cook dinner together, drink wine, and talk into the wee hours. They were taking it slow, still getting to know each other more as friends first before they jumped into anything.

Their relationship was still a secret from their parents and friends. It was something they wanted to protect, for now, but when Clémence walked into work, she couldn't help but exude the happiness that she was feeling.

Celine, one of the hostesses, noticed her glow as soon as she came in through the salon door. She took her break and followed Clémence into the kitchen.

"Something's up with Clémence," she said to Berenice.

"It does look like you're walking on a cloud," Berenice said.

"Where've you been, Clémence?" Sebastien said. "I had to test out my inventions with these inferior taste buds."

"I've been solving crimes," Clémence said. "It takes up my time."

"That was ages ago," said Berenice. "And you haven't been in to work since."

"Something is different about you," said Sebastien. "Are you wearing more makeup?"

"No, nothing. Why can't I just be happy to see you guys? It's been so long."

"It's a boy, isn't it?" Celine said.

"Here we go." Clémence smiled and mock-rolled her eyes. "The boy talk."

"Admit it," Berenice said. "It's a boy. Let me guess, that hot neighbor of yours?"

Even Sebastien was looking at her with an eyebrow raised.

"Okay, fine," Clémence said. "We're dating, okay? His name is Arthur."

"I knew it," Berenice exclaimed. "Didn't we tell you? He couldn't stop staring at you that time we went the La Coquette."

"We all said he was gorgeous," Celine said dreamily. "Didn't I say he was gorgeous? But you said you didn't think so. Classic denial."

"I thought he was cute, but he grew on me, okay? Every time there's a murder, he's around to help me. And we got to know each other a bit more recently. He's not bad."

"Not bad?" Celine said. "Where's the details?"

"What exactly have you been up to?" asked Berenice. "Is he a good kisser? Have you gone all the way? Don't keep all the intimate details to yourself, now."

Clémence blushed. She wasn't going to spill everything, of course, but she was so happy that she couldn't help but gush a little bit.

"From beginning to end," Celine demanded. "When was your first date?"

"Well…" Clémence began.

RECIPE 1: CLASSIC FRENCH BAGUETTES

Makes 2 large baguettes or 4 small ones

French Baguettes have a crunchy crust and a chewy center. If you're in France, you will often see French people carrying these long, thin loaves home after work, often tucked under one arm.

Making gourmet quality French baguettes at home is not as hard as you think.

Ingredients:
- 1/4 tsp. rapid rise yeast
- 1 1/2 cups water, room temperature
- 4 cups all-purpose flour
- 1 3/4 tsp. salt
- 1/2 tsp. cornmeal

In a large mixing bowl, pour in the yeast and stir in the water, then the salt. Add the flour and stir with a wooden spoon until the dough is thick and sticky (5 to 10 minutes). Cover the bowl with plastic wrap. Let it sit in a turned-off oven until it doubles in size, 12 to 14 hours. The dough will be sticky and bubbly.

Dust cornmeal generously on a silicone baking mat on a sheet pan.

Using a floured spatula, scrape out the dough onto a well-floured work surface, and dust dough with flour. Pat dough into a rectangle with well-floured hands, and cut into 4 equal pieces (or 2 if making large baguettes).

Dust each piece of dough with flour. Use floured fingers to gently roll and stretch out into a log. Transfer to the baking sheet. Repeat with other piece(s). Dust loaves lightly with flour. Dust a piece of plastic wrap with flour and drape it lightly over the baking sheet with the floured side down. Let the loaves rise until doubled, 1 to 1.5 hours.

Preheat oven to 500 degrees F or as high as your oven will go. Place an oven-safe baking dish full of water into the bottom of the oven.

Use sharp kitchen shears to cut 4 or 5 angled slashes on the dough. Poke down the sharp tips of dough left by the scissors. Spray loaves with water in a spray bottle.

Bake in the middle rack of the oven until baguettes are browned (15 minutes), spraying loaves with water after 5 minutes and 10 minutes. Turn the pan around after the second spraying.

Transfer the baguettes to a cooling rack. Let cool to room temperature before serving.

RECIPE 2: PAIN DE CAMPAGNE

Makes 2 loaves

Pain de Campagne (Country bread) is a white bread made with a mixture of corn flour and rye flour. The thick crust helps the bread keep longer. You can buy them round (from a French boulangerie) or baguette shaped.

For the Starter:
- 1/2 tsp. instant yeast
- 1/2 cup warm water
- 3/4 cup whole wheat flour

For the Dough:
- 6 cups unbleached bread flour
- 2 1/2 cups warm water

- 1/2 tsp. instant yeast
- 1 tsp. salt
- 2 tbsp. cornmeal for dusting

Whisk the 1/2 tsp. yeast in 1/2 cup warm water. Stir in the whole wheat flour until it turns into a thick batter. Beat for around 100 strokes to form long strands of gluten. Cover the bowl with a damp cloth and let it sit at room temperature for 2 to 8 hours. When it's ready, it will be bubbly and loose.

Scrape it into a bowl and stir in the 2 1/2 cups water and the last 1/2 tsp. of yeast. Stir well. Add bread flour 1 cup at a time, mixing well after each addition, until the dough becomes too difficult to stir.

Put the dough on a floured surface and knead for 10 to 12 minutes. Add more flour only when the dough gets too sticky to handle. Sprinkle salt over the dough and knead for 5 to 7 minutes more. The dough should have a smooth surface and spring back when touched. Shape the dough round and cover with a damp cloth for 5 to 10 minutes.

Put the dough in an oiled bowl, turning it to coat the surface of the dough with oil. Cover dough with a damp cloth. Let rise at room temperature until doubled in size (2 to 3 hours).

Cut dough into two pieces. Shape into two

rounds. Cover them with plastic or a damp cloth. Allow the dough to rest for 30 minutes at room temperature.

Shape the dough into rounds or into long baguettes. Place a heavily floured cloth on a baking sheet, arranging a fold down the center to separate the loaves. Place the loaves on the floured cloth. Dust the top of the loaves with flour. Cover with a damp towel. Let rise until doubled again, about 2 hours.

Preheat oven to 375 degrees F. Sprinkle a baking sheet with oatmeal. Gently transfer risen loaves to the baking sheet. Make diagonal slashes in the loaf with a blade.

Place the loaves in the oven. Bake until golden brown (25 to 30 minutes). Cool loaves on wire racks.

RECIPE 3: PAIN COMPLET

This recipe for Pain Complet (Whole Wheat French Bread) makes one large, country-style round loaf. You can cut the dough to make smaller loaves, or smooth the dough out into elongated shapes to make baguettes.

Ingredients:
- 2 cups whole wheat flour
- 3 cups all-purpose white flour
- 2 cups water, lukewarm
- 1 egg
- 1 tbsp sugar
- 1 tbsp dry active yeast
- 2 tsp. salt

Sift the two flours into a large bowl. Add salt and sugar. Create a large hole in the middle of the mixture to pour in the yeast. Pour 2 cups of lukewarm water over the yeast. Sprinkle a tsp. of flour on top. Wait around 10 minutes for bubbles to appear in the yeast. (If the yeast doesn't bubble, it's no longer active or you didn't use lukewarm water. If that's the case, you'll have to start over.)

Once the bubbles form, mix together all the ingredients by hand to form dough. The easiest way is to gradually incorporate the flour at the sides of the bowl, bit by bit. At the end, it should be a round, firm ball of dough. If it's too sticky, add a bit more flour.

Remove the dough from the bowl and place it on a lightly floured surface. Knead by pushing your palms into and then turning it one quarter. Keep kneading and doing quarter turns for 5 to 10 minutes or until bread is supple and non-sticky.

Place the bread in a lightly floured bowl and cover with a damp cloth. Let rise for 2 hours at room temperature until doubled in size.

Preheat oven to 400 degrees F. Re-sprinkle work surface with flour. Prepare a baking pan by lightly oiling and flouring it, or line with parchment paper. With hands, remove bread and place on surface. Punch down once, hard, with palm. Re-shape into a ball. Put the ball on the baking pan. Use a sharp knife to cut diagonal lines across the top of the bread.

Whisk egg and brush it on top of the bread. Put in oven and bake for about 30 minutes. (Adjust baking time for different sizes.)

RECIPE 4: PAIN DE SEIGLE

Pain de Seigle (Rye Bread) is normally about 70% rye flour mixed with white flour. This rustic French rye bread recipe mixes wheat rye and barley flours flavored with a pain de champagne starter to make a hearty loaf with a chewy crust. It's artisan bread at its best, and it's easy.

For the starter:
- 1 1/4 cup all-purpose flour
- 1/2 cup rye flour
- 1/4 cup barley flour
- 1/2 tsp. sourdough or pain de champagne starter
- 1 1/4 cups water

For the dough:
- 2 1/4 cups all-purpose flour

- •3/4 cup rye flour
- •2 tsp. instant yeast
- •1 1/2 tsp. salt
- •Whole starter
- •2/3 cup water

Stir all the starter ingredients and store, loosely covered, in a warm place (80 degrees F) for 18 to 24 hours.

Stir remaining dry ingredients into the starter and 2/3 cup water. Knead dough for 5 minutes until smooth and elastic. Let rise in a warm, draft-free place for 1.5 hours.

Line a large baking sheet with non-stick foil and turn the dough out onto it. Shape the dough into a large round or oval. Loosely cover and let rise until it has nearly doubled in size.

Preheat oven to 450 degrees F. Spray surface of bread with water. Make 3 diagonal slashes on top of bread and bake for 20 to 25 minutes, until golden brown and sounds hollow when tapped.

Cool rye bread on a wire rack.

RECIPE 5: PÂTÉ AUX POMMES DE TERRE

Here is a fairly simple recipe for a Pâté aux Pommes de Terre, which is like a potato pie and can be served either as a main dish or a side dish. It can also be made with leftover bread dough instead of the puff pastry.

Ingredients:
- 2 puff pastry sheets
- 3 1/2 pounds potatoes
- 1/2 ounce crème fraîche
- 1 large onion
- Salt and pepper
- Egg yolk

Peel and wash the potatoes. Cut into thin strips. Peel and chop the onion. Mix potatoes, salt, and pepper.

Put one of the two puff pastries in the bottom of the pie plate. Fill with potatoes and onion mixture. Add half of the crème fraîche. Cover with the second puff pastry sheet, wielding to the first one. Brush the top with egg yolk. Bake at 400 degrees F for about 1 hour. Serve with rest of the crème fraîche.

ABOUT THE AUTHOR

Harper Lin is a *USA TODAY* bestselling cozy mystery author. When she's not reading or writing mysteries, she loves going to yoga classes, hiking, and hanging out with her family and friends.

For a complete list of her books by series, visit her website.

www.HarperLin.com